Emily Harvale lives in ...
although she would pre...
Alps ... or Canada ...
several months of sn...   ... snow
almost as much as she loves Christmas.

Having worked in the City (London) for several years, Emily returned to her home town of Hastings where she spends her days writing ... and wondering if it will ever snow.

You can contact her via her website, Twitter, Facebook or Instagram.

There is also a Facebook group where fans can chat with Emily about her books, her writing day and life in general. Details can be found on Emily's website.

Author contacts:
www.emilyharvale.com
www.twitter.com/emilyharvale
www.facebook.com/emilyharvalewriter
www.instagram.com/emilyharvale

**

Scan the code above to see all Emily's books on Amazon

Also by this author

The Golf Widows' Club
Sailing Solo
Carole Singer's Christmas
Christmas Wishes
A Slippery Slope
The Perfect Christmas Plan
Be Mine
It Takes Two
Bells and Bows on Mistletoe Row
Just for Christmas

Lizzie Marshall series:
Highland Fling – book 1
Lizzie Marshall's Wedding – book 2

The Goldebury Bay series:
Ninety Days of Summer – book 1
Ninety Steps to Summerhill – book 2
Ninety Days to Christmas – book 3

The Hideaway Down series:
A Christmas Hideaway – book 1
Catch A Falling Star – book 2
Walking on Sunshine – book 3
Dancing in the Rain – book 4

Hall's Cross series
Deck the Halls – book 1
The Starlight Ball – book 2

Michaelmas Bay series
Christmas Secrets in Snowflake Cove – book 1
Blame it on the Moonlight – book 2

ISBN 978-1-909917-67-5

Published by Crescent Gate Publishing

Print edition published worldwide 2020
E-edition published worldwide 2020

Editor Christina Harkness

Cover design by JR and Emily Harvale

Emily Harvale

Just for Christmas

Dear Reader!
Wishing you a very Merry
Christmas and a Happy
New Year!

CRESCENT GATE PUBLISHING

Love
Emily xx

For Ian. Just because.

One

Molly Ford stood at the bright blue door of her brother's quaint, white-washed, thatched cottage and smiled nervously. She tucked a wayward lock of long, golden apricot hair behind her ear and rang the doorbell.

Snow fell softly around her as she waited for Terry to answer and she fixed her gaze on the beautiful wreath, hanging at eye level. Boughs of fresh, forest-green pine festooned with Christmas roses, sprigs of holly, gold-painted pine cones and heavenly scented cinnamon sticks, entwined with a red and gold ribbon, all tied with an oversized bow. It was certainly festive.

No doubt Sarah had made it. Sarah made the majority of the Christmas decorations that now adorned Terry's cottage. And not just the Christmas decorations. Since the day Terry had asked Sarah to move in with him, almost two years ago, she had put her stamp on the picturesque property. She'd made the curtains, the cushions, the throws and quite a bit of the bedding. She was exceptionally talented with a needle, especially one in a sewing machine and she'd used her skills to turn the cottage from a minimalist bachelor pad into a warm and welcoming home.

Terry was not alone in thanking his lucky stars that Sarah had come into his life. Molly was grateful for that day too. She often asked Sarah to make things for her interior-design business, Molly Ford Interiors. Molly might have an eye and a talent for redesigning the inside of any residence, but she was hopeless with a needle and thread and verging on dangerous with a pair of scissors.

Sarah wasn't the only artisan Molly turned to for assistance when it came to creating the perfect home, but Sarah was definitely Molly's preferred choice for all soft furnishings.

That was part of the skill set of a successful interior designer. It wasn't necessarily about what you knew, but who you knew. And Molly knew a number of extremely talented craftspeople and specialists in a variety of skills and trades. She had people she could call on to make absolutely anything her clients might desire, from hand-blown glass lightshades to stained-glass windows; cushions to rugs; door knobs to the very doors they helped open, and ornaments to hand-crafted furniture. The list was endless. If a client wanted it, Molly found a way to source it or have it made, whatever it was. In the four and a half years since she had been running her own business, there hadn't been one unhappy or disappointed client.

That was partly due to people like Sarah Davis. Molly had met Sarah a matter of weeks after starting Molly Ford Interiors. It was at the annual craft market held during July in Easterhill, the town where Molly and Terry had both grown up. Molly, who now lived in Bristol, having moved there with her boyfriend, and stayed after the relationship had ended, was visiting Terry for the weekend.

Sarah had recently moved to Easterhill from London after a bad relationship break-up of her own and was selling cushion covers and other soft furnishings she had made, at one of the market stalls.

Molly fell in love with a William Morris 'Forest' design cushion on Sarah's stall, and in between Sarah serving other customers, the pair chatted for almost an hour about their mutual love of all things, William Morris and similar designers from the Arts and Crafts movement.

They continued their conversation over a cream tea later that afternoon when Sarah took a break, and by the end of the day, when Molly helped Sarah pack up her wares, Molly felt as if she and Sarah had been friends all their lives.

It seemed the most natural thing to do to

ask Sarah to join her and her brother Terry for a drink that evening in the nearby pub, The Piemaker's Rest, which just happened to be at the end of Piemaker's Place, the road where Terry lived.

It might not have been love at first sight between Terry and Sarah, but Molly was convinced that night that it wouldn't be long before the pair became an item. There was definitely a spark. She could see it in the way Terry listened intently to every word Sarah spoke, and the warm smile he gave her repeatedly throughout the evening. And the flush on Sarah's cheek and the frequent surreptitious glances in Terry's direction, assured Molly that Sarah returned his interest.

And she was right, even though Sarah initially told Molly that she felt it was far too soon for her to get involved with another man after her recent break-up.

Molly persuaded Terry to persevere. Not that he needed any persuasion; just a bit of sisterly support and encouragement.

At first he'd offered Sarah friendship and they had met for coffee once or twice a week. After a month or two, Terry reported to Molly that he and Sarah were meeting for the occasional evening drink. They progressed from there to casual dinners every now and then but Sarah still seemed reluctant to commit to anything more than friendship.

Whenever Molly stayed with Terry, Sarah also spent the entire weekend with them and it was clear that Sarah and Terry should be together. Molly was determined to make it happen and, by that Christmas Eve, when Molly finally managed to get them both beneath the mistletoe after several failed attempts, it was obvious to everyone, including the couple themselves that the kiss was going to be the first of many.

They'd started dating the following day and Terry asked Sarah to move in with him two years later.

'You're here!'

Terry flung the door open, with a smile, and stated the obvious. Molly could always count on her brother to do that.

'Yes I am,' she replied, laughing as Terry leant forward to kiss her on the cheek, his ginger fringe flopping across his face.

'Er. Hold on.' He shoved his hair back from his eyes and glanced down at the bedraggled bundle of tan and fawn fur sitting on the doorstep beside Molly. 'That's a dog.'

'Well spotted, Sherlock. I can't get anything past you, can I?'

Terry furrowed dark copper brows and rubbed his stubbled chin between his thumb and forefinger.

'Why have you got a dog? When Belter died, you said you'd never get a dog again because losing him broke your heart.'

'That's true. I did. But I was twelve at the time. And I haven't got a dog. This one's not mine. I'm just looking after him for Christmas.'

Terry looked sceptical.

'You're looking after someone else's dog for Christmas?'

'In a manner of speaking. Do we have to have this conversation on the doorstep? It may have escaped your deductive powers, but it's just started snowing and it's cold out here. Miracle needs to be in the warm. And not just Miracle, I might add. The heating's playing up in my car again and it was distinctly frosty for the last few miles.'

'Miracle?'

'The dog. I've named him Miracle. Because it was a miracle I found him and a miracle he's alive.'

'Right. Er. I'm sure you'll explain all that later, but the thing is, Molly, Sarah's allergic to dogs. Surely you remember that?'

'Damn!'

How could she have forgotten? Sarah would cross the road to avoid an oncoming dog. It wasn't that she didn't like dogs. She did. But if she got within two feet of one, she'd break out in hives and her eyes and nose would run.

It wasn't a pretty sight.

Both Molly and Terry had witnessed it when Terry's good friend, Chance Warren had met them all for coffee one morning, over four years ago now. It was a couple of months after Molly and Sarah had met, and a few months before Terry and Sarah had started dating. Chance had brought his mum's new Olde English Sheepdog puppy, Beauty with him. He'd got it for her as a birthday present.

Sarah, it transpired, hadn't wanted to be rude, so she hadn't mentioned her allergy but within a matter of minutes, the poor girl was a mess.

Chance had done the decent thing and left immediately, much to Molly's disappointment. She'd only seen him a few times since he'd moved back to America with his dad about twenty years earlier, and each time he had looked better than the last.

Molly had had a massive crush on him when he'd been the good-looking, strapping six-foot teenager who'd lived a couple of streets away and that crush had only intensified as Chance had grown into an extremely handsome man.

His chestnut hair seemed richer and darker, his blue eyes more intense and his lopsided smile was definitely sexier.

She'd always thought – or hoped – that one day something might happen between them, but for some reason it never had. Over the years, whenever Chance came to visit his mum, either Molly had a boyfriend or Chance had a girlfriend, but on that particular occasion, both it seemed, were unattached and Molly had high hopes.

But once again, it wasn't to be. She was leaving the next day and so was Chance, Terry had informed her.

She could still remember the smile Chance had given her that day as he and Beauty hurried away. The sort of smile that made her think he might be almost as disappointed as she was that they wouldn't get to spend any time together.

Or perhaps he was merely disappointed not to be spending any time with his mate, Terry. Chance was on a flying visit for his mum's birthday, and whenever he came over to see his mum, he caught up with his childhood best friend.

When Chance and Beauty left that day, Molly had taken Sarah to the ladies. Sarah swallowed down one of her allergy tablets and washed her hands and face and soon after that the runny nose and eyes returned to near normal and the red blotches on her face and neck slowly began to fade. But as Sarah avoided dogs at all costs, Molly hadn't witnessed the effects of Sarah's allergy since then – and had completely forgotten about it.

But she hadn't forgotten about the look Chance had given her that day, even though she hadn't seen him since.

He'd been back to Easterhill several times to visit his mum, and he'd met up with Terry and Sarah, but on every occasion, Molly had been busy with work and hadn't been able to get to Easterhill in time to see him.

More than once, she'd given Terry a good telling off for not letting her know sooner when Chance was coming over. Finally, Sarah had promised to contact Molly herself to let her know. Except Chance hadn't been back for months – until now.

Completely out of the blue, in the first week of December, he arrived in Easterhill and announced to Terry and Sarah that he was moving back for good. Or at least for the foreseeable future.

'He's bought one of the cottages just around the corner from us,' Sarah informed Molly the night Chance had told them his news. 'It's in Wishing Well Lane. He's done it all online and over the phone, apparently, and he didn't want to mention it until the purchase had gone through. He's collecting the keys tomorrow but he told us the place needs doing up.'

'That's fantastic news!' Molly exclaimed. 'Can I come and stay for Christmas?'

Sarah laughed. 'You always come and stay for Christmas, so why should this year be any different?'

'Because this year, I might finally get a

chance with Chance.' Molly quipped.

'Er. Not necessarily. I hadn't finished. I hate to be the bearer of bad news, Molly, but I'm afraid he's got a girlfriend.'

'Oh?' Molly tried not to sound as disappointed as she felt. 'Has she come over with him? Or did he find her online too?' she joked. 'Perhaps he hasn't met her yet. He might be picking her up tomorrow, along with the keys to his new home.'

Sarah laughed again but suddenly became serious. 'I wish that were so, but Terry told me that Chance and Jolene have been dating for a while.'

'Jolene? Her name's Jolene? Isn't there a song about someone called Jolene?'

'Yep. By Dolly Parton, I think. It was one of my mum's favourites.'

Sarah broke into a rendition of the song and Molly moved away from the phone.

Sarah might be exceptionally talented with her hands but she definitely couldn't sing.

'Why are you two standing at the door?'

Sarah's laughter came from near the kitchen and Molly popped her head into the hallway as Terry moved to one side. Sarah was wiping her hands on a Christmassy towel, her auburn hair a tumble of curls, her face a picture of happiness, her cheeks flushed from the warmth inside the cottage, and flour and possibly icing sugar, were splattered down her snowman-patterned apron.

'Er. I'm so, so sorry, Sarah. I completely forgot you're allergic.'

Molly held up the lead that Asher Bryant, a nearby vet and good friend of Terry's, had given her, so that Sarah could see it, and Miracle turned his head from watching the falling snowflakes, to peer into the hall.

'I found him wandering on Easterhill Road,' Molly continued. 'I couldn't believe it at first and I drove past him about three times, back and forth, before I stopped and went over to him. He didn't have a collar or anything and there wasn't anyone in sight. I wasn't sure what to do so I telephoned Asher and he said that if I could get Miracle into my car – that's what I've called him. Miracle. Anyway, if I got Miracle to Asher's surgery, he'd check the microchip and contact the owner. Dogs have to be chipped now by law, apparently. But there wasn't a chip, so we couldn't find out if anyone owns him or where he came from. Asher reported it to the local council, to let the dog warden know – which is another legal requirement and he called the local shelters and the RSPCA but they were all inundated. I know I shouldn't have, but as no one had any room for him, and I've owned a dog before, I offered to look after him. Just for Christmas. Asher cleared it with the powers that be and I knew Terry wouldn't mind. I didn't think you would either. Honestly, I completely forgot about your allergy. Truly I did. Now I don't know what to do. I'll have to take Miracle back to Asher and see if he can find someone else to look after the poor thing.'

Asher Bryant lived in a tiny village by the sea, about fifteen miles south of Easterhill. It was called Seahorse Harbour and was a pretty magical place. Molly had often thought it was the perfect place to live. But so did everyone else, it seemed, and property there rarely came on to the market, either for sale or to rent.

Asher and Terry had met two years ago, via their mutual love of running. They'd bumped into one another several times on their respective runs. Both in their mid-thirties at the time, and with many other interests in common, including each having only one sister, they soon struck up an easy friendship.

Not long after they met, Terry even set up a date for Asher and Molly, but although they enjoyed each other's company, that spark was missing and they'd agreed to be just friends.

Despite the fact that there was at least one vet in Easterhill, Molly had called Asher and driven the extra miles out of her way because she trusted him completely. Both with people and with animals.

Sarah sniffed.

Her allergy was clearly starting already and Miracle was nowhere near her yet. Molly couldn't ask her to let Miracle stay. Not even for just one night.

'Well, you can't spend the night out there,' Sarah said, half laughing, half sighing. 'I'll go and take one of my tablets and we'll see what happens. But please try and keep him as far away from me as possible.'

'You're letting him stay?'

Molly couldn't quite believe it. Sarah was a lovely person, Molly knew that, but to allow the dog to stay even though it meant she would suffer was really going above and beyond.

'Yes. But just the dog. You can find somewhere else to stay.' Sarah laughed at her joke before sneezing loudly and dashing off, no doubt to take her allergy tablet.

Terry frowned at Molly as he let her in.

'How could you have forgotten? If Sarah's tablets don't help, you're going to have to take the dog elsewhere, you know that don't you?'

'Of course. I'm sorry. I wasn't thinking. But what could I do? I couldn't leave him by the road, could I? And Asher tried really hard to find a place for him, but everywhere is full to bursting. I'd offered before I even realised what I was doing. And even Asher must've forgotten about Sarah's allergies, so it wasn't just me.'

Miracle sniffed the Christmas themed doormat, the door, and Terry's legs before glancing up at Terry as if to say, 'Hello. Who are you?'

Terry sighed. 'He's a bit of a scruffy mutt but he doesn't seem the worse for his adventure,' he said, closing the front door and bending down to pet Miracle. 'He could very well be a stray and not belong to anyone. Look at the expression on his face though. It sort of says, "Whatever". He doesn't appear to be at all concerned by any of this.'

Miracle promptly licked Terry's face before shaking vigorously and sending wet snow everywhere. He flopped onto the floor and scratched behind his ear with his back paw, shook his head again and yawned as if he was bored.

'Asher said something similar.'

Molly dropped the lead that Asher had given her. He'd also given Miracle a Christmassy collar and the dog hadn't been at all bothered by that, so although Miracle wasn't tagged and his details hadn't linked up with any on the 'missing animals' websites, both Asher and Molly felt it might not be the first collar Miracle had ever worn. Either he had belonged to someone at some stage in his young life, or he was so laid back that absolutely nothing fazed him. Asher told Molly he thought the dog was about two.

She shrugged off her coat which Terry took from her, but before she had time to retrieve the lead, Miracle suddenly opened his eyes as wide as saucers, sniffed the air enthusiastically and darted off towards the kitchen.

Molly and Terry shot a look at one another and chased him along the hall. They arrived in the kitchen just a few seconds after him, but they were too late to save the honeyed ham.

Miracle had taken a large chunk out of it and both his cheeks were crammed with meat. He sat, with a saintly expression on his face, as if he hadn't done anything wrong, despite the fact that the remnants of the ham lay on the floor in front of him between his large paws.

'Miracle!' Molly snapped but couldn't stop herself from laughing as the dog tried to chew on his bounty without making it obvious he was doing so.

'It's not funny.' Terry didn't sound amused in the least. 'Sarah's spent the whole day cooking that, and all for nothing.'

'Not entirely for nothing. Miracle seems to be enjoying it.'

Terry scowled at her. 'I hope you'll still be laughing when you're eating cheese and biscuits tonight because your dog's eaten the ham.'

'I love cheese and biscuits.' Molly winked at her brother and gave him a playful nudge. 'I'll go and buy a ready cooked ham and I'll apologise to Sarah. It's not the end of the world, Terry.'

Miracle pushed the ham behind him and turned his back so that they couldn't see him devour more of it. Now, Terry did laugh.

'Does he really think we can't see what he's doing? He's not very bright, is he?'

Molly laughed louder. 'I don't know about that. He's the one eating honeyed ham for supper while we'll be having cheese and biscuits. That's pretty smart of him.'

Two

Chance Warren gazed at the now pale rose-white, double fronted, thatched-roof cottage, with a sense of achievement. Only a few weeks ago, when he'd become its debatably proud owner, he had seriously wondered if he'd made a mistake. He'd heard of 'buyer's remorse' and it was definitely possible that at that time, it was exactly what he was feeling. The cottage then was a vivid cerise pink, and far more dilapidated than it had looked on the internet.

He'd had a survey, of course. One of his old friends had carried it out. But when he'd collected the keys after completion, he realised that perhaps he should've taken more notice when Phil, the surveyor had laughed and asked him if he'd lost his mind.

'It might be cheaper to knock the place down and build a new one,' Phil had said.

'It doesn't look that bad in the photos,' Chance had pointed out.

'Photos can be deceiving, mate. You only

have to see some of the girls I've dated from those online dating sites to realise that. They're nothing like their pictures. And Wishing Well Cottage is nothing like the photos on the estate agent's site. Now I'm not saying they've been photoshopped or anything, but they must've been taken a long time ago. And through a rose-tinted lens on a bright sunny day.'

'Is it really that bad?' Chance had tried to hide his disappointment. 'Don't forget I'm a builder. I can turn my hand to most repairs.'

'There's damp. Plaster's fallen off most of the walls in places. The wooden window frames are rotting. The kitchen's out of the forties and don't get me started on the bathroom.'

'But is it structurally sound?'

'Well, there's no sign of subsidence and the place has stood for a couple of hundred years and could well be there for a couple of hundred more, but it needs a lot of work. And didn't you say you want to have the place refurbished by New Year's Eve? I don't think there's much chance of that, mate. Not without a miracle. But it does have a couple of surprisingly ornate fireplaces and some other original features. With time, a lot of effort and a large amount of money, the place could be transformed.'

'Then it's good that I've got all three of those things, isn't it?' Chance felt happier at that moment and had decided to press ahead, but when he'd first seen it in reality, he'd definitely had some doubts.

Now, as he looked at the pale rose-white façade, toned down several shades from the eye-piercing pink of old, an immense sense of pride soared through him. Even his buddy Phil couldn't believe the transformation. Phil had been right though; the place had taken a lot of time, effort and money to bring out its true potential.

Chance, along with a team of plasterers, carpenters, electricians and plumbers, most of whom were friends of his or Terry's, had virtually gutted the place.

All the old plaster had been removed from the internal walls, the damp treated, and the walls replastered. The external walls had been repaired, the brickwork repointed where necessary, and the façade repainted.

Ceilings, which were either falling down or covered in polystyrene tiles, swirls of Artex or even psychedelic artwork, had been repaired, replastered or replaced.

The old kitchen had been ripped out, along with the ground floor bathroom, and an extension with a glass roof and vaulted ceiling had been added. Top of the range kitchen furniture in a pale grey, and luxury fittings and appliances had been installed, together with a boiling water tap. The floor had been levelled, concreted, and covered with dark grey, polished Travertine tiles.

Elsewhere, in the small hall, and the sitting and dining rooms, the oak floorboards had been sanded and polished.

Upstairs, one of the four bedrooms had been converted into a luxury bathroom with pristine white, high-end design furniture and fittings. A free-standing bath, a spacious walk-in shower, and a raised toilet and vanity and sink unit gleamed on the marble tiled floor.

The remaining three bedrooms and the hall, together with the stairs would be carpeted with an expensive wool blend, but Chance hadn't yet decided on a colour. All the internal doors were painted in a pale ivory satinwood.

The cottage had been rewired and all the ancient light fittings replaced but at the moment, only bulbs hung from the wires. Chance was good at all things connected with building works but interior design left him cold.

When the majority of the refurbishment work was completed, he'd shown his mum around and asked if she had any ideas, but frankly, Vicky Warren was as bad as her son and now he was starting to get anxious. He was running out of time. It was the eighteenth of December and he had just under two weeks to get the place ready in time for New Year's Eve. He couldn't miss that deadline.

'You could paint everything off-white to match the doors,' Vicky had suggested.

'It's pale ivory, Mum,' he'd replied.

Ignoring him, Vicky continued: 'And the crystal chandeliers we've got in our house would look nice. Although the ceilings here are lower, aren't they? But they'd be fine in the vaulted ceiling of the kitchen extension.'

Vicky had always referred to her house as 'our house' even though Chance didn't live with her but with his father in the States. Chance loved that fact – although he didn't love the chandeliers. They were about as 'crystal' as he was. But acrylic chandeliers didn't have the same 'ring' to them; he fully appreciated that.

'I think chandeliers might be a bit out of place in a cottage, Mum. But I'll give it some thought.'

'You know who you need, don't you?' Vicky said, as they left the cottage and walked the few steps to his car.

'Who?'

She grinned at him. 'Molly Ford!'

Of course. Why hadn't he thought of that? Molly was an interior designer. She even had her own business. But there was only one problem. She lived in Bristol.

'I don't know why I didn't think of her.' Chance shook his head and laughed. 'I wonder if she'll be coming to stay with Terry this Christmas. If not, I suppose we might be able to do something over the internet. I could upload photos and she could upload her design suggestions. I'll nip round to Terry's this evening and ask if he thinks she'd be up for that.'

Vicky smiled. 'There, you see. I told you I could help.'

Chance gently wrapped an arm around her shoulder and gave her a loving smile.

'And you've done so much more than you can imagine. Thanks, Mum. Now let's get you home in the warm and out of this snow. You need to rest.'

'Pah!' Vicky tutted. 'I'll rest when I'm dead. It's Christmas, darling, and if this is my last one, I want it to be the best Christmas it can be. And this cottage is part of that. You finally moving back here is a dream come true for me.'

'It won't be your last.'

He hadn't meant to snap but he couldn't bear to think of that.

'Maybe, or maybe not. We'll have to wait and see. But I don't want you worrying about me, you hear? I want you to have fun this Christmas. I want to see that gorgeous smile of yours, and hear that melodic laugh. You've already changed all your plans for me. You should be spending Christmas with Jolene, skiing in Vermont and staying with her parents. Instead you're here, putting the finishing touches to this wonderful cottage that you've spent the last few weeks doing up, just so that you could spend time with me. I adore you for that. Well, I adore you anyway, but more so for giving up so much for me.'

'I haven't given up anything. I wanted to be here with you. And Jolene and I will have every Christmas together for the rest of our lives, so one doesn't matter.'

Vicky hesitated. 'You're certain she's The One, then?'

Was he?

Was he really certain of anything right now?

Other than that he had wanted to move back to England and to live near his mum and to make her happier than she'd been for a long time. He wanted her to have the opportunity to be at his wedding. That was something she often told him she dreamt of. Something she wanted more than anything. To see him settled and happy and married to the perfect woman.

Jolene was definitely that. She was almost too perfect. Sometimes he looked at her porcelain complexion and realised he couldn't remember the last time he'd seen her without make-up. Although the make-up Jolene wore made it seem as if she wasn't wearing any. That's how perfect it was.

And she was the perfect girlfriend. Beautiful, intelligent, loving and kind. He only had to ask and Jolene would fulfil his every need. When he'd said he intended to move back to the UK for the foreseeable future so that he could spend more time with his mum, Jolene hadn't batted an eyelid. She'd offered to come with him, or not – whatever he wanted she would do, she'd said.

That was when the idea struck him. Perhaps he should propose? Why not? They'd been dating for about a year. They were happy. He hadn't intended to ask her to move in with him in New York, but if he moved back to Easterhill, he couldn't expect her to join him there, but to have to find a place of her own to live.

When his mum had mentioned that Wishing Well Cottage, the former home of someone she had known, was on the market, he hadn't hesitated for a second. He'd looked at the place online, made an offer, and instructed solicitors that day.

He'd told Jolene some of his plans that night and she'd seemed pleased for him. When he'd mentioned that he'd be happy if she'd like to come over to the UK and stay with him, she'd told him she'd like nothing more. She had savings and she'd always wanted to visit the UK. She hadn't asked on what basis she'd be joining him. She hadn't mentioned a visa. Perhaps she'd thought he only intended for them to stay in England for a while. He had been born in the UK, to an English mother and an American father, so he had dual nationality. If Jolene wanted to remain in England for more than six months, she would need a visa. She hadn't even asked where they'd be living, and she hadn't yet seen Wishing Well Cottage.

And he hadn't yet proposed.

He'd thought it would be easy but it turned out that it wasn't. He'd gone as far as buying a ring – which wasn't as exciting as he'd expected it to be, and he wasn't even sure she'd like it. It was a diamond solitaire which had cost him a small fortune. He hadn't minded the expense but he had minded the store clerk wittering on about 'True Love' the entire time he was there.

Was there such a thing? He doubted that very much. People fell in love and they fell out of love. They were lucky if they managed to make their relationship last. The divorce rate soared each year.

What was important was to find someone you liked; someone you got along with; someone who didn't make you want to chew your arm off rather than spend all day with them.

He had that with Jolene. He felt comfortable with her. They never argued. She let him live his life without trying to change him. She never questioned where their relationship was going. She never made demands. She always looked incredible. And the sex was pretty good. Not mind-blowing, exactly, but sex wasn't everything, was it? He thought it could be better, but they could work on that. He was fairly sure he loved her. He definitely liked her a lot.

Chance sighed softly and shrugged.

'As certain as I can be. We've been together for over a year now, and it works. We're comfortable with one another.'

'Comfortable?' Vicky looked horrified. 'Oh dear, darling. Love should be so much more than that.'

'It is. I'm just not very good at explaining it.'

'Hmm. Your father was the same. Until he fell head over heels in love with someone else. He managed to explain that pretty well.' Vicky sighed. 'But I don't blame him. I was awful to him. And to you. I'll never forgive myself for that.'

'There's nothing to forgive, Mum. You were ill. You didn't really know what you were doing. And you got the help you needed.'

'Eventually. But far too late. I ruined everything.'

'That's in the past. Even Dad admits that it wasn't entirely your fault. He spent too many hours chasing his career. He didn't see the signs. He didn't talk to you about how you were feeling. But you survived. That's what's important. You beat alcohol addiction and you can beat this cancer. I know it in my heart.'

She stopped and turned to face him, brushing a lock of his chestnut brown hair behind his ear. He took her hand in his, and kissed it.

Vicky gave a tiny cough. 'You need a haircut, darling.'

He grinned. 'It's on my list. But it's not that near the top. When the rest of the guys start wolf-whistling at me, I'll know it's time to make it a priority.'

She shook her head and laughed. 'It's been a long time since anyone wolf-whistled at me.' She sucked in a breath. 'You're right, darling. I can beat this cancer. And now that you're going to be living just around the corner from Beauty and me, I couldn't ask for anything more.' She glanced down at the four-year-old, Olde English Sheepdog standing patiently beside her and patted the dog's mass of white and grey fur. 'Let's go home and get Beauty in the warm. We can have a mug of hot chocolate. And maybe a mince pie. An alcohol-free one for me, of course.'

Three

Terry sounded both surprised and pleased as he opened the front door. And so was Molly when she heard the hint of an English-American accent.

'Is that Chance?' she mouthed across the room to Sarah, whose eyes were getting more watery by the minute, in spite of both Molly and Miracle sitting as far away from her as possible.

Sarah sneezed loudly before nodding. 'Sounds like it.'

'Hey!' Chance was saying. 'I hope it's okay for me to drop by.'

'Of course it is. Come in. Sarah? Molly? Chance is here.'

Molly grinned at Sarah and jumped to her feet. Sarah hauled herself off the sofa, sneezed like a foghorn, and dropped back onto the cushion.

'Sorry to intrude, Sarah,' Chance began, but as he caught sight of Sarah, he stopped talking and stood still, furrowing his dark brows. 'Are you okay? Have you got a cold or something?' He shot a brief glance in Molly's direction, looked surprised, but smiled awkwardly and returned his attention to Sarah.

'Allergies,' Sarah croaked and pointed towards Miracle who sat at Molly's feet, apparently oblivious to the distress he was causing.

'Oh yeah. You're allergic to dogs I seem to recall.'

'Glad someone remembered.' Terry glowered at Molly.

'I said I'm sorry.' Molly threw her brother a sulky glare. 'Hi Chance. It's lovely to see you again. As you can tell, I've brought a dog with me and Sarah is slowly and very bravely, dying.' A thought occurred to her. 'Your mum's got a dog, hasn't she? I don't suppose she'd be interested in looking after Miracle here, would she? Just for tonight. Or even better, just until I can find somewhere else for him to stay. All the shelters were full and I couldn't leave him by the road, could I?'

Chance was clearly confused as his gaze shot between her, her brother, and Sarah, whose eyes were now streaming.

He was also twice as gorgeous as he had been the last time Molly had seen him.

His chestnut hair was longer, curling over his blue scarf towards his coat collar giving him a more laid-back look than before. His eyes were a slightly deeper blue. Or perhaps Molly was imagining that. The lopsided smile seemed more endearing, his voice sounded sexier, he even appeared a little taller and broader somehow.

'Er. Run that by me again. Are you saying the dog isn't yours?'

'Exactly. I found him wandering by the side of the road.'

'And you brought him here?'

'Yes. But I took him to Asher first. You know Asher, don't you? Terry's friend, the vet, who lives in Seahorse Harbour.'

'Yes. I know Asher. Isn't he microchipped?'

'Asher?' Molly grinned.

Chance grinned back. 'The dog.'

Terry tutted. 'It's not a time for jokes, Molly. Look at Sarah. She's a complete mess.'

'Thanks!' Sarah tutted even louder.

'Sorry, angel. You know I didn't mean that the way it sounded.' Terry hurried to Sarah and gave her a kiss on her head.

Sarah rolled her eyes but a look of horror swept across her face and her mouth fell open. Everyone followed her line of sight and Molly gasped in surprise.

Miracle had got up without any of them noticing and was peeing on the stunningly gorgeous, real pine Christmas tree which had pride of place in the corner of the sitting room, to the left of the real log fire.

'Miracle!' Molly exclaimed, dashing over to him and trying in vain to grab his collar.

Miracle barked and playfully leapt in the air before disappearing behind the abundant branches.

Molly heard the rip of paper before anyone else and lunged forward in an attempt to grab any part of the mischievous dog that she could reach, but all she managed to do was lose her footing and she and the tree landed on the carpet in a heap of smashed ornaments and broken branches.

Terry, who had stepped forward to help catch Miracle, stopped in his tracks and stood open-mouthed.

Miracle raced towards the hall with a shredded sheet of wrapping paper, a length of torn ribbon and what looked like a pair of socks, hanging from his mouth.

'Whoa, boy,' Chance said, half laughing as he caught the wayward dog.

'My tree,' Sarah croaked, her voice a little above a rasp.

'I hope you're happy, Molly,' Terry snapped, yanking Molly to her feet. 'You've managed to wreck Christmas in just one night!'

'Oww. Oww. Oww.' Molly picked pine needles from her hands and neck.

Terry pulled a twisted star ornament from her golden apricot locks, taking a few strands of hair with it.

'Oww!' she yelled again. 'You did that on purpose.'

Sarah gave an almighty sneeze. The dog was now closer to her than he had been all evening.

'I've got to go to bed,' she said, rising from the sofa as if she were in a trance.

'You've got to find somewhere else for that bloody mutt to stay,' Terry said. 'And right this minute, I wouldn't mind if you went with him.' He turned abruptly away and hurried back towards his girlfriend. 'Are you okay, angel? Can I get you anything?'

Sarah shook her head and raised her hand in a, 'no thanks' gesture.

Terry grimaced at Chance and glowered at Miracle who dropped the remnants of the paper, ribbon and socks and turned his head away with an expression of innocence on his face, as if butter wouldn't melt in his mouth.

'Sorry about this, mate,' Terry said to Chance. 'I'll just be a minute or two. Keep a tight hold of him, will you?' He nodded down at Miracle.

'Absolutely.' Chance looked as though he were trying hard not to laugh.

'I'm really sorry, Sarah,' Molly yelled as both Sarah and Terry disappeared towards the stairs.

Chance sniggered once they were out of

earshot.

'You certainly know how to make yourself welcome. You're clearly not the flavour of the month right now.'

'No kidding, Sherlock. Well, don't just stand there. Give me a hand with this tree, will you?'

'Er. I would. But I need to keep a hold of this terror.' He patted Miracle's head.

'Don't pet him! He's a naughty boy. A very naughty boy. Now what am I going to do? I think Terry was half serious about kicking me out as well as the dog.'

'Can you blame him?' Chance was still grinning.

'I didn't pee on the tree! Or wreck the place. Or eat the honeyed ham.'

Chance raised his brows and roared with laughter. 'He ate a ham?'

'Yep. Within five seconds of arriving.'

'Tell me again why he's here with you.' Chance tied the lead to either side of the door handle so that Miracle couldn't wriggle it free. 'Sit and stay.'

Molly was astonished to see Miracle sat at Chance's command and was delighted when Chance crossed the room in three easy strides, hauled the tree upright and fixed it back in place.

She regaled him with the story while he gathered up the broken ornaments and placed them in the hearth. Molly rearranged the ribbons and bows and with Chance's help they rehung the lights. By the time she had finished her tale, having gone into detail about her drive here, seeing Miracle, catching him and getting him to Asher's and how many calls Asher had made once they discovered the dog wasn't microchipped, the tree didn't look that bad. All things considered.

'It's another miracle,' Molly said, smiling at Chance.

She felt guilty but oddly proud that they had managed to salvage the gorgeous tree, even though it didn't look quite as gorgeous now. But there was something in the way Chance was looking at her that made her tummy do a somersault.

'You're right,' he said, a hint of wonderment in his voice. 'It is a miracle. And a miracle is just what I needed. You want to find your dog a place to stay, and I want you. How do you feel about coming to stay with me?'

'W-what?'

Now this really was a miracle. Had Chance just said he wanted her? Had he just asked if she wanted to go and stay with him? This was a dream come true.

'Oh my God, Chance! Yes! I'd love to.'

He seemed a bit surprised that she was so effusive. Had he just taken a small step back or did she imagine that?

'Er. I should warn you, there are strings attached.'

'That's fine. I don't mind strings. Wait. As long as it's nothing kinky. I'm not into that.'

'Kinky? No. Why would you think that? Just modern. Top of the range. Price is no object.'

'Price? What ... what do you mean by price?'

Was he offering to pay her? And what the hell was "top of the range"? He wasn't asking her to have sex with him on top of his cooker, was he?

'I mean you can spend as much as you like. I want to bring the pages of one of those posh magazines to life. Especially in the bedroom. And I'm sure you're an expert in your field. Terry and Sarah sing your praises, as does Mum. I don't know why it didn't occur to me. But it was actually Mum who suggested you'd be perfect.'

Molly closed her eyes for a second and shook her head. Perhaps her tumble into the tree had addled her brain.

'I think I might be missing something. I'm a little confused. When you said you wanted me, what exactly did you mean?'

He looked perplexed for a second before his brows shot up. 'Oh. Er. I didn't mean...' He gave a nervous laugh. 'I've just bought a cottage that I'm doing up. I'm fine with all the building work but when it comes to the interior decoration, I'm at a total loss. You're an interior designer. I could really use your expertise.'

'My expertise? To design the interior of your cottage? That's it?'

'Yes.'

'I see.' She forced a small chuckle and a smile. 'Of course that's it. I knew that's what you meant. I was teasing.' She bit down her disappointment.

'Don't worry, Molly. You'll be perfectly safe with me. I know it's a lot to ask. And I'm on a time limit too. My girlfriend's joining me here on New Year's Eve. I haven't told anyone this, apart from Mum, but I'm planning a surprise proposal so I need to have the cottage finished before she arrives. I'm hoping she'll want to stay for good. What do you say, Molly? Will you help me out in return for a place for you and Miracle to stay for Christmas? I'll even look after him while you come back here to spend time with Terry and Sarah. I think this could be the perfect solution for us all.'

Four

It certainly seemed to be the perfect solution as far as Terry was concerned. And no doubt Sarah, although as she was sneezing, coughing and wheezing upstairs in her bed when Molly broke the news to Terry, Molly couldn't ask her.

'You know I love you, sis,' Terry said, an expression of pure joy and utter relief brightening his face, 'but this does seem like a perfect plan for everyone. We'll still get to spend Christmas together – without the dog – and Chance will get his cottage finished in time for New Year's Eve.'

Molly glanced at Chance and, as if he read her mind, he gave a slight shake of his head. He hadn't told Terry the reason why he wanted it to be ready by then. She wondered why he had told her. Perhaps it was because of the misunderstanding. Maybe he wanted her to know he was taken and that she didn't have a hope in hell of getting as much as a kiss from him, let alone full-on sex.

And she had hoped. Just a little. Oh okay. A lot. She'd had a crush on Chance for years and tonight, for just one brief, magical moment, she thought he was actually saying he felt the same. Or at the very least, that he wanted a holiday fling with her. But nope. That wasn't what Chance wanted at all. All he wanted from her was her time and her talent for design.

Oh well. That was better than nothing. Wasn't it? And Chance was an old friend. The least she could do was help him out in his time of need.

Besides, she didn't really have a choice, did she? If she wanted to keep a roof over Miracle's head – and she definitely did want that – she'd have to find somewhere else to stay. Chance's offer was the best she was likely to get.

Asher would probably take her in if she asked him to, but he was expecting his sister and their parents for the holidays. He'd told her that today. His cottage wasn't exactly huge, especially as his veterinary practice took up part of it, so it wouldn't be fair to dump herself on his good nature. Although, if the weather continued as it was, his family might not make it.

No. It was mean-spirited to even think those thoughts. Asher deserved a good Christmas. He was such a lovely guy.

And so was Chance. In fact, Chance was

more than lovely. Chance was positively gorgeous. Chance was almost god-like. Chance was ... a problem.

Could she really stay with him and not be tempted to climb into his bed? Or flirt with him? Or try to get him interested in her?

Of course she could. She was annoyed at herself for thinking otherwise. She was a grown woman in her thirties, not some silly, fifteen-year-old. And she wasn't so desperate for love that she'd actually try to 'steal' another woman's boyfriend. Even if it had been a couple of years since she'd had a boyfriend of her own.

She simply wasn't thinking straight right now. Today had been weird in so many ways, what with driving all the way from Bristol and arriving in the snow, saving Miracle, only to discover there was no room in a shelter, and inflicting mayhem and madness on her brother and Sarah one week before Christmas.

She and Miracle would go and stay with Chance. She would ensure his cottage was worthy of the cover of the best house-style magazine. She would give his girlfriend – and soon-to-be fiancée, a dreamlike place to live. She would enjoy a lovely, relaxed Christmas with her brother and Sarah, and she would find Miracle a home before she returned to Bristol in the New Year.

And she would finally get over her childish

crush on Chance Warren. He was now taken, once and for all.

There were plenty more fish in the sea. She simply needed to find some new waters to swim in because all she had found up to now, was a lot of frogs.

Five

Wishing Well Cottage wasn't at all as Molly had imagined.

For one thing, it already looked as if it had won first prize in a home refurbishment competition, and wasn't even slightly run-down in any way. She knew Chance had been doing it up but for some reason she had assumed that would still be ongoing. She hadn't expected the pristine, blank canvas she saw when Chance opened the newly-painted, warm-grey, front door and switched on the light in the hall.

For another thing, the place was exactly that: a blank canvas. As Chance led the way she noticed there wasn't a stick of furniture to be seen, apart from one battered and paint-splattered wooden chair, looking somewhat lost and lonely in the middle of the sitting room.

'It's gorgeous, Chance. It really is. I'm truly impressed.'

He beamed at her. 'Thanks. That means a lot.'

'Just one tiny question.'

'Shoot.'

'Er. Where is the furniture?'

'There isn't any.'

'None at all?'

'Nope.'

'None upstairs, either?'

He shook his head and his chestnut hair shone beneath the bare lightbulb hanging above his six-foot frame.

Why didn't that seem to bother him?

'Er. Isn't that a problem?'

'Yep. But that's where you come in. I told you. I'm hopeless when it comes to interiors. I seriously need some help.'

Molly sucked in a breath.

'I won't argue with that. But what I meant was, I was rather hoping for a bed. Or at least a blow-up mattress. Am I going to have to sleep on the floor?'

Chance looked confused before suddenly bursting out laughing and shaking his head more vigorously.

'I wouldn't ask you to do that, Molly. I still remember the night we went camping. You, me and Terry, in your parents' garden. You flatly refused to sleep on the ground. Even in a sleeping bag. "It's hard", you said. Nothing we could say or do would persuade you and you went back inside to your comfy bed.'

How had he remembered that?

She cleared her throat and threw him a sarcastic smile.

'In my defence, I was only about five at the time. And I loved that bed. It was in the shape of a fairy-tale castle and the mattress was as soft as a cloud. I thought the grass would be softer, like it is in summer. Besides, it wasn't a great idea to camp out in the middle of December. I don't know why Mum and Dad allowed it.'

Chance grinned. 'It was Christmas Eve. And I think they allowed it because they knew none of us would stay out there for long. It was absolutely freezing. But you're forgetting it was your suggestion.'

'It was? I don't remember that.'

He shook his head again, still grinning. 'Selective memory, I think that's called. You wanted to see Father Christmas in his sleigh, racing across the night sky with his reindeer. We made a make-shift tent out of old blankets, and a huge piece of plastic sheeting from the rolls that my dad used on his building sites. We sellotaped it to the blankets with your Fairy Princess tape, but that didn't work so your dad stapled the plastic to the blankets. He made a wooden frame and voilà! One tent. We'd have got soaked if it had rained, and buried if it had snowed, but you went back indoors after five minutes and said you'd watch for Santa from the window. Terry and I lasted for about an hour. Your mum called us in for hot chocolate before you went to bed, and we caved.'

Molly laughed. 'Wow! I can't believe you remember all that. Although you were four years older, so maybe it had more of an impact on your memory than it did on mine.'

'I remember a lot from those days. You were really bossy, I remember that.'

'I was not!'

He raised his brows and chuckled. 'The lady doth protest too much. You were, Molly, and you know it. The term, 'high-maintenance' was coined for you. You made Terry and me do all sorts of crazy things for you. And we did them. Willingly. You had special powers, obviously. You could get us to do whatever you wanted.'

'I wish I had those powers now.'

Rats! She hadn't meant to say that out loud.

He tipped his head to one side. 'Don't you?'

'Nope. I can't get anyone to do anything I want these days.' She saw an odd look in his eyes and changed the subject slightly. 'I still miss Mum and Dad. We both do. Mum always made Christmas magical.'

'She did.' Chance's voice held a note of tenderness. 'I truly loved your parents and I envied you and Terry. I don't know if I ever told you that after your parents died.'

Molly shook her head. 'No. But I knew you were almost as upset as we were. The first few years were the worst, of course, but time's a great healer and they've been gone for more than half my life. Now when I think of them, it's with happy thoughts and only the occasional tear. I know your parents made your life difficult when you were young, but you're lucky to have them both.' She gave a cough. 'But back to the point in question. If there isn't any furniture but you're not going to ask me to sleep on the floor, where, exactly, will I be sleeping?'

Chance was giving her another very strange look. This time as if he wanted to say something but wasn't sure if he should.

'Didn't I say? I thought I had. At Mum's. Don't look so worried. I know I should've checked with her before I made the offer, but I did call and ask her while you went upstairs to get your things, and she was more than happy about it. She's always liked you. And you like her, don't you?'

'Of course! Your mum's great now. I mean. Er. She always was.'

'There's no need to pretend, Molly. We both know she was a nightmare when we were young. But she's changed a lot over the years and she often tells me that you stop and chat for ages whenever you bump into her. I know you even helped her buy a birthday present for me the first year after Dad and I left for the States. It was a navy-blue sweater and a *Star Wars* book.'

'Did she tell you I helped?'

Vicky must have told him. How else would he have known? But boy, did he have a good memory. Suddenly, she wondered if she'd ever done anything she would rather he had forgotten.

'Yep. And I still have them both, as it happens. Although the sweater doesn't fit. I've bulked out a bit since my teens. Navy blue was my favourite colour. It still is.'

'I know. Well, I knew it was then. And I knew how mad you were about the whole *Star Wars* thing.'

He frowned. 'Excuse me? "*Star Wars* thing"? How dare you!' She could see he was trying not to laugh. 'It's not a thing. It's a religion.'

'Yeah, right. Whatever floats your boat. Or should that be, whatever flies your star ship?'

They both laughed until Molly heard a crash and they met each other's eyes.

'What was that?' she asked.

'No idea. Where's Miracle?'

Without another word they both darted in the direction of the noise.

Six

'Are you beginning to regret your offer?'

Molly held Miracle's lead tightly while Chance got on his hands and knees and cleared up the mess.

'Perhaps a little.'

But he said it with a smile, albeit a somewhat wan one.

'I'll pay for the damage,' Molly offered.

'No need. I shouldn't have put a Christmas tree up anyway. The place is empty, after all. I just wanted a bit of festive sparkle while I worked. No harm done. Thank God I put it up in the kitchen. And that I laid the tiled floor. Pee is easier to clean off tiles than it is from polished wood floors.'

'I'm not going to ask you how you know that. But it's probably a good thing that the tiles have that mottled effect. If they were a plain grey, you might still notice the pee stain. And I think we can – and must, assume that Miracle has a thing about Christmas trees.'

'Oh yeah. I'd better warn Mum. She's got three at home.'

'Three trees? Wow! And I thought I was a Christmas nutter. Oh God. I didn't mean ... Er. I seem to be saying all the wrong things tonight, don't I?' She grinned sheepishly.

'Mum won't mind being called a Christmas nutter. In fact, she'd be the first to admit it, so don't worry about that. You don't need to feel you're treading on eggshells where Mum and I are concerned, Molly. You've known us far too long for that.'

She let out a sigh. 'That's a relief. I must admit I'm a bit nervous about staying at your mum's. If I'd known that, I might not have said yes so fast. Not that there's anything wrong ... Okay. I think I'll just shut up now.'

He glanced up at her from the floor and grinned.

'I think that would probably be a first, wouldn't it? You always liked to talk. But there's no reason to be nervous. Mum's happy about it. Honestly.'

'It's silly, I know, but I'm never good with my boyfriend's mums. Oh! Not that I'm saying you're my boyfriend. Because you're not. Obviously. And you've got a girlfriend anyway. Oh hell. Here I go again. Er. Did you tell your mum about Miracle?'

He was giving her a very odd look, but he rolled his eyes and laughed at that.

I mentioned that you'd got a dog. Temporarily. And how you got him. But I didn't mention the tree. Now I'll have to. I don't think she'll mind. She's pretty easy going these days. She often says ...'

His voice trailed off.

'She often says what?' Molly coaxed.

He ran a hand through his hair and sighed loudly as if he carried a heavy load.

'That life is for living and for having fun and who cares if you cause a bit of havoc now and then?'

'Hmm. She hasn't met Miracle yet. But then again, we could all do with a miracle in our lives. Sometimes we have to run with what we're given and hope for the best.'

He got to his feet and looked her directly in the eye. He was close enough for her to smell his aftershave and she breathed it in. A mixture of sandalwood and pine. Or maybe the pine was from the tree.

'If I tell you something, Molly, will you promise me that you'll keep it a secret? That you won't tell anyone else. Not even Terry or Sarah.'

She held his gaze and hesitated. There was a deep sadness in his eyes and he was clearly hurting.

'Yes. Of course. What's wrong, Chance?'

Instinctively, she reached out and touched his hand.

The bolt of electricity she felt was unexpected and from the sudden lift of his head and the surprise in his eyes, he felt it too.

It must've been caused by static or something. Except they were standing on a tiled floor.

She pulled her hand away and waited for him to speak.

'Er. I...'

He coughed, and coughed again, as if something had caught in his throat and his eyes scanned hers as though he were searching for something deep inside her.

'You can trust me, Chance,' she managed.

His gaze intensified.

'I know I can, Molly. It's just that...' He coughed again. 'Okay. Mum has been having tests recently and it wasn't looking good. That's why I've come home. The day before I bought this place, she was diagnosed with breast cancer.'

'Oh, Chance. I'm so, so sorry.' She wanted to reach out to him again but she stopped herself. 'It's not too late though, is it? I mean they have said they can operate, haven't they?'

He nodded. 'At first they thought it was just a small lump in one breast but the scans have shown another slightly larger lump in the other one. She's having a double mastectomy in the first week of January. That's the earliest they can do it.'

'That's just a few weeks away. And she'll be fine, I'm sure. Lots of women have breast cancer, and the majority survive if it's found in time. It might not seem like it but the operation is a good thing, Chance.'

He nodded. 'I know it is. And I know she'll get through it. But sometimes a tiny flicker of doubt creeps in. When she finally told me how bad it was, after dismissing it for days, I told her I was coming home to live with her. She said I had a life to live and not to worry about her. That the last thing she needed was me getting under her feet on a permanent or semi-permanent basis. She tried to make light of it. That's why I bought the cottage. She couldn't argue with that. Although at first she did.' He gave a half-laugh. 'But the thing with Mum is that she doesn't have a lot of luck. She's partly convinced herself that this is it. That this Christmas will be her last. And I can't help wondering if she's keeping something from me. That she hasn't been completely truthful about what the consultant has said. Sorry to be so morbid, but I thought, as you're staying with us, perhaps you should know the score.'

'I'm glad you've told me. And I'll keep it to myself. Not even Vicky will know that I know. But she's wrong, Chance. This won't be her last Christmas. It won't. She'll have loads more after this one. We just need to convince her of that.'

He let out a long, slow sigh. 'You don't know what a relief it is to have told you. I was struggling with it on my own. I promise I won't burden you with my worries, but it is good to know that I'm not totally alone.'

'Of course you're not. And you won't be burdening me. Feel free to share your worries, doubts and fears whenever you need to. That's what friends are for. It must be difficult being so far away from your girlfriend. You must miss her comfort and support.'

'Er. Jolene doesn't know. I haven't told her yet. You're the first person I've told. Jolene just knows that Mum has been unwell and that I want to spend some time with her.'

Molly was gobsmacked to say the least.

He hadn't seen her for years and yet he'd chosen to tell her and not his girlfriend about his mum. That was a bit weird, wasn't it? But perhaps he'd only told her because, as he'd said, she was staying with them.

Or maybe it helped to talk to someone who wasn't quite so close, so involved.

Yet Molly felt involved. She wanted to hug Chance and his mum and tell them both everything would be fine.

And it would.

Cancer terrified everybody. For good reason in many cases. But so many people were beating it these days. Vicky Warren would be one of those. Molly was sure of it.

'It's Christmas, Chance. And Christmas is a time for miracles.'

He smiled at her. 'I hope you're right.'

Miracle let out a sudden bark, almost as if he agreed. And then he peed again on the Christmas tree that Chance had just brought back to life.

Clearly, some miracles were better than others.

Seven

'Molly!'

Vicky Warren beamed at Molly and stretched out her arms for a hug, but Molly stepped away.

'I'm covered from head to foot in snow, Mrs Warren. It's really coming down out there.'

'Oh Pah. I don't care about that.' She pulled Molly into a tight embrace.

'Mum,' Chance said. 'I think Molly may be having trouble breathing. You don't know your own strength.'

He was only joking but Molly was glad when Vicky released her. The woman did have the grip of a vice even if she looked more like a twig. She had definitely lost weight since the last time Molly had seen her and her porcelain skin had a slightly sallow tinge.

But she still looked beautiful. Her hair was now short and spiky in place of the once shoulder length bob and the glorious chestnut colour had turned a silvery grey. She obviously no longer had it coloured, but it suited her. She had elfin features, unlike Chance, but he had inherited her stunningly blue eyes. She was shorter than Chance by about six inches: the same as Molly in fact, but she held herself with an almost Regal air which somehow made her seem taller.

'You're looking gorgeous, as always,' Vicky said, unperturbed. 'I was so pleased when Chance said you were going to be staying with us for a while. And how kind of you to take in a stray dog. But then you always had a kind heart. It's such a shame Sarah is allergic. But their loss is our gain. And this must be the terror in question.'

'Thank you so much for having me. You're looking gorgeous too. That hair colour and style really suit you. And yes. This is Miracle.'

Vicky turned her attention to Miracle who was sitting beside Molly giving Beauty, Vicky's Olde English Sheepdog a look as if he was wondering whether Beauty was a dog or a rug.

Molly hoped Miracle didn't suddenly decide to pee on Beauty. Or try to eat her as he had the ham. Or rip her to shreds like he had the presents.

'Hello, you handsome boy.' Vicky bent down to pet him. 'Yes, you're a handsome boy. Yes, you are.'

Molly lifted her gaze from Vicky to Chance and met his eyes, returning the smile he was giving her.

'We think you should know that he seems to have a bit of a thing for trees,' Chance told his mum. 'Christmas trees in particular.'

'And hide the ham if you have any,' Molly added, laughing. 'He's rather partial to that, too.'

'And presents,' Chance said. 'So basically, we'll need to keep a close eye on him.'

'He looks quite young.' Vicky continued to pet Miracle.

'Asher, the vet I took him to, thinks he's about two,' Molly said.

'Ah yes. The terrible twos.' Miracle nuzzled closer to Vicky. He seemed to be enjoying himself.

'Isn't that for children?' Molly queried.

Vicky grinned and shrugged. 'He's so lovable. If he's a stray he's possibly just trying to get attention. Some people say it's seven human years to every dog year, so that would make him a teenager. Teenagers are always trouble. Apart from you darling, of course.' She smiled at Chance. 'You were no trouble at all. I was the one who was playing up.'

Chance coughed as if he didn't want to go there. 'I'll make us some tea.' He deposited Molly's case at the foot of the stairs.

'I'm sure Molly would prefer a glass of wine, darling.'

'No.' Molly may have said that too hastily.

She knew about Vicky's history. She'd seen the woman drunk on more than one occasion, many years ago. 'Tea's great.'

Vicky smiled. 'It's fine, Molly. I honestly don't mind. I never liked wine anyway. I was a Scotch kind of girl. I bought some wine for my friends as it's Christmas, so there're are some bottles in the cupboard.'

'Thanks, Mrs Warren, but I'd prefer a cup of tea.'

Chance threw her a grateful smile and wandered off towards the kitchen.

'Call me Vicky, sweetheart. Mrs Warren sounds so old and formal, especially as you're staying with us. Now come and sit, and tell me, is there a man in your life? And if so, where is he?'

Molly sat on the sofa and Miracle sauntered over and flopped at her feet, eyeing Beauty who was slowly edging over towards the stranger in her midst. Miracle stood up again and he and Beauty sniffed one another as Molly held his lead as tight as she could. Just in case. But Miracle soon curled up at her feet again and Beauty wandered over to Vicky, jumped up next to her on the loveseat and dropped onto Vicky's lap.

Vicky laughed merrily. 'She's done this since the day Chance bought her for me, but she seems to forget that she's about five times the size she was then. Probably more.'

But Vicky threw an arm around Beauty and cuddled her tightly while she licked Vicky's face.

'She clearly adores you,' Molly said. 'And in answer to your question, no. There's no man in my life at the moment.'

Which wasn't strictly true. There was Chance.

Although he wasn't hers.

But he was in her life. Very much so, she was just beginning to realise.

She'd have to knock her feelings for him on the head or she'd be starting the New Year with a broken heart.

And she definitely didn't want that.

Eight

'I'm so, so sorry about yesterday, Sarah,' Molly said into her phone as she stretched in the comfort of the guest bed at Vicky's house. 'How are you feeling this morning?'

'Much better thanks. Which is just as well as I need to go and do some Christmas shopping. I've got a pair of socks and a few other presents to replace.'

'Ah. Yes. Sorry about that too. And the ham. And everything really. You'll be pleased to know – or maybe not, that Miracle also devastated a tree Chance had in his kitchen in the cottage, and peed on it as well. Twice. So it wasn't just yours. Chance had put it up to make the place feel festive. He'd be better off putting some furniture in there, to be honest, but I guess that's my job.'

'I'm not sure that makes me feel any better. Has Miracle wrecked anything at Mrs Warren's yet?'

'Surprisingly not. But then again I kept a

tight hold of him all evening. He did nearly pull me off a chair while we were having supper, but that was because I'd wrapped his lead around the leg of it and when he tried to dash off after something, he almost took me with him. Chance managed to grab me, the chair and amazingly Miracle too, and saved the day. He spent the night with me, but I tied him to the bed.'

'Who spent the night with you, tied to the bed? Chance or the dog?'

'Funny. I wish it had been Chance, but sadly not. And Miracle is currently snoring away beside me. May I go Christmas shopping with you? I'll pay to replace the stuff Miracle ruined.'

'Yes, of course you can come. And don't be so bloody stupid. You don't need to pay for anything. I'll tell you what. Buy me a Latte and a mince pie and we'll call it quits.'

'Deal.'

'What time will you be free? I assume you'll be at the cottage for much of today.'

'Oh. I suppose I will. I'd forgotten about that.'

Sarah laughed. 'I wonder about you sometimes, Molly. I'd like to go this morning if possible. It's still snowing and I don't want to be coming home in the dark in this weather.'

'Okay. I'll ask Chance at breakfast what his plans are and let you know.'

'Perfect. Oh! I almost forgot. Asher phoned Terry earlier to arrange to meet up for a run. He told Terry he's met someone! Can you believe it? He met her yesterday. Not long after you'd left his surgery. He was out for a run and he bumped into her. Not literally. She was walking her spaniel and looking in a shop window as he approached. He said he thinks he made her jump. She probably thought he was a mugger or something. He stopped and chatted to her and he told Terry that there was something about her he really liked. He had no idea what, but he felt something. As if she's going to be important in his life, somehow. He said that when she smiled at him, he felt as if he'd won the lottery. Which is apt really, because her name's Lottie, apparently.'

'That's Christmas magic!' Molly exclaimed. 'I'm so pleased for him. He deserves to meet someone special. I hope it works out. And I wish I could get some of that. All I end up with is a mangy old dog who destroys every Christmas tree he meets.'

'You'll find someone special soon, Molly. I know you will. And Asher might not have found his 'True Love'. She told him she's only in Seahorse Harbour for the holidays, visiting an aunt. We'll have to wait and see. So how're things going with Chance?'

'They're not. Not in the way you mean. We're just friends. You were right about his girlfriend. And it sounds pretty serious. I'll have to cross Chance off my 'things I want for Christmas' list. Oh, hold on. I think he might be at the door. Can I call you later?'

'Absolutely.'

Molly rang off and sat up in bed, covering her brushed cotton, polar bear-patterned pyjamas with the duvet.

'Come in.'

Vicky popped her head around the door and beamed at Molly, and Miracle suddenly opened one eye and lifted his head from the bed.

'Good morning, sunshine. And good morning you gorgeous boy. Did you sleep well?'

Molly wasn't sure if that question was for her or the dog but Miracle seemed to assume it was for him because he barked twice, as if to say, 'Yes thanks'.

'Like a log,' Molly said, not wanting to be outdone by a dog.

'You up yet, Molly?' Chance called from the hall. 'I've brought you a mug of coffee.'

'She's sitting up,' Vicky said. 'And she's decent. I hope you've got one for me.'

Vicky stepped aside, and Chance marched in, handing one of the mugs to Vicky as he passed by. She reached out and pulled him to her, kissing him on the cheek.

'Careful! You nearly made me spill it.'

Vicky grinned and winked at Molly, who

was trying to cover her pyjamas once again so that Chance wouldn't see them.

'Thanks, Chance. But you didn't need to do this. I was just about to get up.'

'It's no trouble. Great PJs, by the way.'

He was already dressed in faded jeans, a navy-blue T-shirt and a slightly lighter blue, V-necked sweater.

He handed Molly the mug and as she moved to take it from him, Miracle stretched, rolled over onto his back and let out an almighty fart. A very smelly one.

'Oh my God!' Molly pinched her nostrils together with two fingers of one hand, and held the mug of coffee with the other.

'That was probably the honeyed ham he stole,' Chance said, laughing.

Another fart escaped and this was so loud it even made Miracle jump. As he leapt from the bed, he knocked Molly's arm and the coffee sloshed all down the front of her pyjamas.

She let out a shriek. The coffee wasn't just wet, it was hot. She virtually threw the now half-empty mug at Chance who managed to grab it with one hand, as she yanked her top away from her bare and slightly scorched skin. But as she did so, the buttons popped open and she gave both Chance and Vicky, who was loitering in the doorway, an eyeful.

Miracle was still tied by his lead and he careered back towards the bed as though he were a boomerang. His rear end thumped against Chance, who was already off-balance due to saving the mug. Chance stumbled and fell, landing awkwardly on top of Molly.

Molly felt Chance's hand brush her breast before he flopped beside her, the remnants of the coffee in the mug he still held, splashing over them both. All she could hear, as she blushed profusely and cursed under her breath, was Vicky's raucous laughter and Miracle's playful bark.

Chance pushed himself off the bed and grinned sheepishly. 'Sorry about that. I blame the dog.'

'If that bloody dog makes it to Christmas it'll be a miracle,' Molly snapped, tugging each side of her pyjama top together while Miracle licked trickles of coffee from the duvet.

Nine

Saturday hadn't got off to a good start but Molly was determined it would improve. It couldn't get any worse. Could it? Although with Miracle around, anything was possible.

Vicky's breakfast certainly helped. It was a long time since Molly had eaten a Full English, along with orange juice, toast, butter and marmalade.

Chance hardly said a word but every so often Molly caught him looking at her, a furrow in his brow.

'What's on the itinerary today?' she asked, in an attempt to end his awkward silence. 'I'd like to go Christmas shopping with Sarah at some stage, if that's okay, but I'll fit in with you as much as possible. It does mean that I'll be throwing myself on your mercy and asking you to look after Miracle for a couple of hours though. I can't take him with me. He'll probably decimate the shopping centre.'

Chance grinned at that. 'Why don't you go

shopping this morning and we'll work at the cottage this afternoon? I'll take him and Beauty for a long walk while you're at the shops. That might tire him out. Especially as there's several inches of snow out there. Would that fit in with your plans?'

'Perfectly. Are you sure you don't mind?'

'Not at all.' His grin widened. 'But ask me again later.'

Molly grinned back and glanced at Miracle who was standing beside Beauty munching down his breakfast and slowly edging his bowl closer to hers, no doubt in the hope that he could steal some of her food without her noticing.

'I'll wash your PJs,' Vicky said, 'and when they're dry, I'll re-sew some of the buttonholes so they're not so wide. If you've got anything else to go in the wash, let me have it before you go out.'

Molly blushed at the memory of earlier.

'Thanks. But there's really no need. I can do that later.'

'You can sew?' Chance sounded doubtful. 'I'm sure Terry said you weren't very good with a needle and positively lethal with a pair of scissors.'

Molly tutted and tried to avoid his gaze. 'You shouldn't believe everything my brother says.'

'So that's not true?'

She blushed deeper. 'Er. No. Or yes. It is true. But I'm sure I can sew a few buttonholes.'

'But you don't have to, sweetheart,' Vicky insisted. 'I'm happy to do it. So that's that.'

There was no point in arguing. Especially as Molly really didn't want to do any sewing. The last time she attempted that, it ended with a trip to A&E and four stitches. Scissors were definitely not her friend.

'I've already got a few ideas for the cottage,' she said, changing the subject. 'I'm thinking hand-blown glass pendant lights in three colours to go above the kitchen island, hanging from that fabulous oak beam you installed. I know someone who makes the most gorgeous shades and the glass looks so delicate but is actually quite sturdy. I'm seeing one gold shade, one amber and one vermilion. And I'm picturing something like maybe an inverted teardrop, with the widest part at the top, narrowing at the bottom so it looks as if the glass is melting onto the hob that you've built into the island.'

'I love that!' Chance beamed at her. 'So basically, yellow, orange and red?'

'Heathen.' Molly playfully slapped his arm. 'Gold isn't yellow, amber isn't orange, and vermilion isn't red. They're all so much more and come in a variety of hues. Some soft, some strong. But I think a splash of bright colour will highlight the dark grey floor tiles and the pale grey units. Have you decided on the splashback? Last night you said you were considering grey glass, but what about amber or vermilion to really make a statement? And to add more colour. Or maybe two-tone, with vermilion at the base fading into pale amber at the top? Or glass tiles to match the pendants?'

Vicky tapped Chance's hand. 'I love the idea of those lights, darling, and a two-tone splashback sounds wonderful. The kitchen looks superb but with some added colour, it would look sensational.'

Chance nodded. 'I agree.'

'I think the sitting room needs deep, bold colours. I haven't decided on those yet. But last night I was thinking about your bedroom.' She cleared her throat. She'd been thinking about his bedroom quite a bit. But it had nothing to do with the colour scheme. She'd actually dreamt about being in bed with him, and it had been so vivid that when she first woke up, she half expected to find him sleeping next to her. Instead, she'd been face-to-slobbery jowl with a snoring dog. 'Umm. I know how much you love blue, especially the darker tones like navy, so what if you paint those superb built-in wardrobes of yours a deep, rich blue, with maybe a soft pink for the walls to add more warmth?'

'The deep blue wardrobes sound good, but pink walls?' Chance pulled a face. 'I know pink is your favourite colour, Molly, or at least it was, but I'm not sure I can see myself in a pink bedroom.' He grinned.

'I think it sounds lovely,' Vicky said, eyeing them over her coffee.

'Don't think pink as in candyfloss,' Molly said. 'Think of the colour of … setting plaster. That's a manly pink.'

'Setting plaster?' Chance thought about it. 'Now that sounds cool. And I can picture that with the dark wardrobes.'

'Excellent. Now you said you wanted the bedroom to look like something in a magazine, so I'm thinking, luxury hotel. What about a bedframe with a dark blue, padded, buttoned, high headboard? The bedding would be layers of the blue of the bed, the wardrobes and the pink walls. With maybe a touch of deep magenta. A throw and perhaps one cushion? And I think the bedside lamps should make a statement. I'll work on that. And go with me here. What if you painted the ceiling a midnight blue and had a few, subtle, tiny stars dotted here and there? With those two large roof lights you've added, it would seem as if the entire room were open to the night sky. Or is that going a bit too far for you? Picture yourself lying on that bed, looking up at the stars.'

He didn't respond immediately and she wondered if he was having second thoughts about wanting her help, but there was something in the way he was looking at her that made her skin tingle and her heart race.

When she'd pictured that bedroom, she'd imagined being in his arms, staring up at a black velvet sky sparkling with a myriad of stars. Was he imagining something similar? Except he would be seeing his girlfriend in his arms, not her.

'I think I need to get you to redesign my bedroom,' Vicky said. 'That sounds heavenly, doesn't it darling?'

Chance swallowed and his voice cracked when he spoke, so much so that he coughed once he'd managed, 'It does.'

'So you like it?' Molly was delighted.

He nodded and held her gaze. 'I can picture it right now. It ... it's perfect.'

'That's great. I can pick up some paint samples while I'm out, and I'm sure Sarah can supply a lot of the soft furnishings I have in mind. I was going to suggest you build a window seat in that side bay window. We could have cushions to match, or to complement the bedding. And perhaps wooden shutters the same colour as the wardrobes. Imagine sitting opposite one another reading a book. It's big enough for two. Or drinking a glass of wine, watching the snow falling outside. Isn't that romantic? Oh! ... Er ... When I said 'we', I meant that in the designer and client sense, obviously.'

'Of course you did, sweetheart.' Vicky didn't sound convinced and the huge grin added to that.

Chance didn't say a word. He ran a hand through his hair and coughed again.

Had she embarrassed him?

'I think that's enough for now,' she said. 'I'd better call Sarah and see what time we can meet. When do you want me back, Chance?'

'Sorry. What?'

'What time do you want me to be at the cottage?'

'Oh. Er. Whenever. What about straight after lunch? Say, two o'clock?'

'Perfect.' Molly glanced at her watch. 'It's a little after nine, so that gives me plenty of time to spend some money. And some of that will be yours, Chance. I just thought I should mention that.'

He grinned. 'What's mine is yours.'

A hint of colour crept across his clean-shaven face and a little thrill ran through Molly, but she damped it down. He had a girlfriend. A girlfriend who would very soon be his fiancée. She must remember that.

And she must stop designing his cottage as if she were going to be living there. That was a definite no-no. And extremely unprofessional. She'd never done that before. But then she'd never designed anything for Chance Warren – until now.

'And what's mine is yours,' she joked, nodding towards Miracle.

Having finished his breakfast, he was sitting beside his bowl, looking a little spaced out. Almost as if he were in a trance. The calm before the storm she felt, and the sooner she left him to Chance's care, the better her day would be.

'Why do I get the feeling that I've got the worst part of this exchange?'

Molly laughed. 'Probably because you have. Thanks for breakfast, Vicky. I'll call Sarah and then I'll wash up.'

'No need, sweetheart. Chance bought me a dishwasher a few years ago. You go and have fun. We'll take care of this.'

'You're the best,' Molly said, giving Vicky an impromptu kiss on the cheek.

She had no idea why she'd done that. But it was too late to take it back.

Thankfully, Vicky seemed pleased, and as Chance was smiling at them both as if he approved, no harm was done.

But Molly would have to be careful. She was forgetting the reason she was here. And she kept forgetting Chance was as good as engaged, even though she tried to remind herself every fifteen seconds.

'Oh,' she said, suddenly stopping at the door and turning to face Chance. 'I can't believe I haven't asked, but what's your girlfriend's favourite colour?'

Chance blinked a few times and frowned, casting his eyes down towards the table. A second or two later he shook his head and met Molly's look.

'Er. I have absolutely no idea. I'll call her today and ask.'

Molly hesitated for a moment, before nodding and dashing off, calling out a final goodbye as she grabbed her coat from the hall, even before she had called Sarah.

Ten

Chance cursed under his breath as he tramped through the snow, virtually dragging two reluctant dogs behind him.

What the hell was the matter with him? Ever since he'd seen Molly at Terry's house last night, he'd been behaving like a teenager with a crush.

It must be because he was tired. Exhausted, in fact. He'd been working on the cottage almost non-stop, between spending time with his mum and worrying endlessly about her. He needed a rest.

Perhaps it was because he was missing Jolene.

Except he wasn't.

He did think about her from time to time, mainly after she had called him for a chat, or after they had Face Timed, but other than that, he rarely thought of her.

That was a bit worrying, wasn't it? Shouldn't you be constantly thinking about the woman you loved? The woman you were about to propose to. The woman you'd be spending the rest of your life with.

But what was even more worrying was the fact that when Molly had described her vision for the kitchen this morning, it was her he had pictured sitting on a stool at the end of that island while he poured them glasses of wine and the pendant lights lit up the hints of red in her golden apricot hair and the flecks of green in her beautiful, hazel eyes.

He entered Easterhill Park, part of the Easterhill Estate that was left to the town by the former owners. The Easterhill Estate had been huge and in addition to this park there was also an air club and a small air strip just outside of the town. Lord Easterhill had a bit of a penchant for planes but when he and his wife died, leaving no heirs, they left the airstrip and the planes to the town of Easterhill and it was turned into an air club, open to anyone and everyone who lived in Easterhill or the nearby Seahorse Harbour.

The modest stately home of Easterhill was sold to a developer and in addition to converting that into a luxury hotel and equally luxurious spa, he eventually managed to obtain permission to use part of the grounds for a golf club. So now the grounds of the Estate were divided between that and the air club and this part of the grounds formed the public

Easterhill Park.

Chance let Beauty and Miracle off their leads. The snow here was pristine. They were clearly the first to venture into the park, which was a bit surprising for a Saturday morning, especially as it was almost ten o'clock. But the heavy snowfall had no doubt kept many in the warmth of their homes, probably sitting by the fire with a mug of hot chocolate, or a cup of coffee.

'Shit!'

He cursed out loud. Why did he have to think about coffee? Now all he could picture was the glimpse he'd had of Molly's breast when her PJs had popped open that morning. And the feel of her silken skin as his hand had brushed against it.

He ran his hand through his hair and sighed.

Worse still, when she'd spoken of her vision for the bedroom, and lying on that bed looking up at the stars, it was Molly he'd seen lying naked beside him beneath the duvet. Not Jolene.

What would Molly look like naked?

What would it feel like to kiss her and run his hands all over…?

This was bad.

This was serious.

This was stupid.

'Stop it, you utter jerk.'

'I'm sorry. Were you speaking to me?'

An elderly woman stood a few feet away, a shocked expression on her kind-looking but wrinkled face. He hadn't noticed her until now.

'What? No. No, I'm sorry.' He gave her a foolish grin. 'I was telling myself off for something. Sorry again.'

She smiled and nodded. 'Girlfriend?'

'Sorry?'

'Is it something to do with your girlfriend?'

'How did you know I've got a girlfriend?'

The woman laughed and shook her head.

'A good-looking man like you? Of course you've got a girlfriend. Maybe more than one. Although I hope not. You look like a lovely young man and no one likes a cheat. You're not, are you?'

'A cheat? No. Not yet.'

'Not yet?'

'Not ever. I hope. I'm not the type. At least I didn't think I was.'

He let out a loud, short sigh.

'Love can make us do things we never thought we would.' The woman smiled wistfully. 'Believe me, I know. Would you like to talk about it?'

'I don't know what I'd say. I'm feeling somewhat confused. I think it's just because I've being overdoing things and need a rest. I've recently moved back here from the States to be with my mum. My girlfriend's still in New York.

I'm supposed to be proposing when she gets here on New Year's Eve. But now someone's come back into my life and I'm feeling things I never felt before. Never expected to feel. And definitely not about her. She's a pain in the butt. Or she used to be. But she's ... Sorry.' He laughed awkwardly. 'I don't know why I blurted all that out.'

'Perhaps because you needed to. I'm old and my husband passed away several years ago, but we were married for more than sixty years and one thing I'm sure about as far as Love is concerned is that you know when it's real. I mean truly real. True Love. You feel it in your blood. You sense it in every breath you take. You see it in every look. If one of them makes you feel as if you can fly without wings, or that without her smile, your world would be plunged into darkness, she's the one.' She reached out and touched his arm, giving him a warm and friendly smile, until her mouth fell open and her eyes peered past him into the distance. 'Good gracious. Is that your dog swimming in that icy pond?'

Chance knew it was Miracle without even looking.

'In a manner of speaking, yes.' He glanced over his shoulder. 'He belongs to the woman I think I may have feelings for. It was lovely to meet you. And thank you for your advice. I'd better go and rescue her dog. Not that he looks like he needs rescuing.'

'No. He seems to be having a whale of a time chasing those ducks. Good luck with everything. And Merry Christmas.'

'Merry Christmas to you too.'

He'd almost forgotten it was less than a week away as he raced off towards the freezing pond where Beauty sat at the edge, looking as if she were grinning.

Eleven

'You girls clearly had a good time.' Chance eyed the number of bags in the back of Terry's Land Rover. 'Did you go too?'

Terry rolled his eyes. 'No. Thankfully. Sarah just asked me to pick them up because they couldn't get a cab and they had too many bags to carry on a bus. I couldn't believe it when I saw how much they'd bought.' Terry grinned. 'I'm glad most of this is coming out of your pocket and not mine.'

'Really? Oh joy of joys.'

'Wait until you see what I've got for you,' Molly enthused. 'You'll love me forever. Oh. In a friendly way. Not a romantic one. Obviously. Er. Have you changed clothes? You weren't wearing those dark jeans and that Christmassy jumper earlier.'

Chance sighed. 'Miracle decided I needed a change.'

'Miracle? Oh dear. What did he do? He didn't pee on you or something, did he?'

'And you're giggling because...?' Chance raised his brows. 'No. Your delightful dog didn't pee on me. He took me for a swim.'

'A swim?' Molly bit her lower lip. She was clearly trying not to laugh. 'Where?'

'The partially frozen pond in Easterhill Park. It was ... bracing, to put it mildly.'

Sarah laughed but suddenly became serious. 'Is he okay? I may be allergic but I'd hate to think anything bad had happened to him. Where is he? I'm not sniffing at all.'

'Oh God!' Molly grabbed Chance's arm. 'Is he hurt? Has he–?'

'He's fine, Molly.' Chance took her hand in his and squeezed it, abruptly dropping it and stuffing his hands in his pockets. 'I left him curled up asleep beside Beauty, on an old duvet Mum had. They're both in the conservatory at Mum's and she's happy looking after them.'

Molly sighed with relief but Chance noticed she was staring at her hand. The hand he'd held.

Had she felt the spark of electricity he'd felt?

That was the second time it had happened.

'So why the swim?' Terry asked, slapping Chance on the back.

'Because Miracle wouldn't come out, no matter how much I called him. And he was basically terrorising the ducks. Not that he managed to catch any. I was worried he'd end up with hypothermia or something. So I really had no choice.'

'You went in and got him?' Molly's eyes opened wide.

She had really beautiful eyes.

'What? Yeah. But he didn't want to come out right away so we ... sort of splashed about for a while until the park warden came and yelled at us and hauled us both out with a long pole. Which was just as well as I was starting to lose all feeling in my legs. I don't think I can venture into Easterhill Park for a few weeks. And Miracle is banned.'

Molly's laugh was like Christmas bells.

'Oh, Chance. I'm so sorry. I bet you're regretting your offer now.'

'No. I'm actually not. Right. Let's get these things inside. Are you two staying? Or do you need to dash off?'

Sarah and Terry exchanged looks.

'We're happy to stay and help if there's anything we can do.'

'There's plenty to do,' Chance said. 'Far more than I realised, in fact.'

'Will you get it all done in time?' Terry asked. 'For New Year's Eve?'

Chance glanced at Molly before quickly turning away.

'That's the plan. And I definitely need some help for that to happen. In more ways than one.'

'What do you mean by "in more ways than one"?' Terry queried.

'Nothing, buddy. Just thinking aloud. Grab some bags and follow me.'

'I've got some paint samples,' Molly said, as they all went inside. 'If we try them out in the bedroom and sitting room today, you'll be able to see what the colours look like under electric light, in the semi-darkness of the evening, and tomorrow, in daylight. I believe it's important to check them out under all forms of light. It's amazing how much they can vary from a rainy day to a sunny one, and in daylight and electric light.'

'I don't think we'll get to see them in the sunshine,' Chance said. 'They're forecasting bad weather for the next few days. Probably more snow.'

'I love snow.'

Molly's face lit up like a child's as she placed her bags on the floor.

Sarah deposited hers beside Molly's and clapped her hands together.

'That'll mean The Piemaker's Rest will be able to hold the annual 'Snowball Pie' event, using real snow for once.'

'What's the Snowball Pie event?' Chance had spent a few Christmases in Easterhill, but usually only for a couple of days, and he'd never heard of that. 'And what do they usually use instead of snow?'

'Balls,' Terry said, grinning. 'Tennis balls usually, or those small plastic ones you can get for dogs. Everyone lines up outside in the garden, in teams of two. One team member holds a tinfoil baking tray in front of them, which is supposed to be the pie, and the other team member stands about ten feet away and has to pick up and throw as many 'snowballs' into the 'pie' as quickly as possible in two minutes. The winners are the team that gets the most balls in the pie.'

'The balls bounce out,' Molly said. 'With real snowballs, more should stay put.'

'Or break up completely,' Chance suggested.

'Ah, but that's the skill,' Terry said. 'Throwing real snowballs at the right speed to ensure they don't. It hasn't snowed at Christmas since Sarah moved here, but Molly and I remember the times it did.'

'Yes.' Molly stuck her chin in the air. 'And Terry and I were the champion Snowball Pie makers for several years in a row. I think I've still got the keyrings to prove it.'

'Congratulations.' Chance grinned at her. 'You're clearly multi-talented. Were keyrings the grand prize?'

'Keyrings in the shape of pies, with The Piemaker's Rest written on them and with a small, fluffy snowman attached.'

'Just what every man needs,' Chance said.

'Remind me to enter this year.'

'You and Molly can be a team.' Sarah sounded excited. 'Against me and Terry. And all the other teams, of course.'

Chance met Molly's glance and grinned. 'I'm up for that.'

'You'd better take it seriously,' Molly said, with a partial grin. 'I'm in it to win. And it's for a good cause. Every team pays to enter and the spectators pay to bet on how many balls the winners will get in their pie. All the proceeds go to a local Children's Hospice. So keep that sarcasm under wraps, Mister, if you want to be on my team.'

'No more sarcasm from me, I promise.' He meant that sincerely. 'When does this take place?'

'On the twenty-second,' Sarah said. 'Which is this coming Tuesday.'

'Great. I'll put it in my diary.' Chance took his phone from the back pocket of his jeans and entered the words, 'Snowball Pie – Pub' on his calendar. 'There. That's a date. Oh. Er. Not a date kind of date.'

'I know what you mean,' Molly said. 'Don't worry.'

Terry and Sarah were giving him odd looks and he quickly changed the subject.

'Okay. Let's get these paint samples done. And I'd like to get some ideas about furniture. I realised today that with the Christmas break,

85

I might be cutting it close with delivery times.'

Sarah tutted. 'You'll be lucky if you can get anything delivered before Christmas, and if we do have bad weather, deliveries between Christmas and New Year's Eve might be delayed. Why didn't you order your furniture sooner?'

'Because he needed Molly's help,' Terry replied. 'Only he didn't realise he needed it until yesterday. We men don't think about stuff like that.'

'Now I *am* worried.' Chance looked at Molly. 'I will be able to get the important things, won't I?'

'Like a bed, you mean?' A crimson blush swept over her face. 'And a table and chairs. A sofa. A TV. A couple of chests of drawers. Some things should be fine if we buy them from one of the local, independent stores. At least you've already got a Range fitted in the kitchen, along with all your white goods, so that's something.'

'And a hot water tap. So I don't need a kettle.' He grinned at her. 'I do need pots and pans and mugs and such though.'

Molly returned his grin. 'Those things we can definitely get locally. Let's make a list. Why don't you and Terry go and apply the paint samples while Sarah and I sit in the kitchen and write out your list? You don't have any chairs, apart from one old battered thing, so you won't mind us sitting on the kitchen counters, will you?'

A vision of Molly perched on his kitchen counter popped into his head. She was wearing her PJs and her top was open.

'Chance? Did you hear me?'

'What? Oh yes. That's fine.'

'Don't you need Chance to tell you what he wants?' Terry asked.

Molly shook her head and smiled, and as her long golden apricot locks danced around her shoulders, Chance felt a flame flicker inside him.

'Nope. I'll check it with you later, Chance, but I think I know exactly what you want.'

He doubted that.

He doubted that very much indeed.

Partly because he wasn't entirely sure himself exactly what he wanted.

Although he did know that right now, it had nothing to do with furniture, or anything else for the cottage.

Twelve

'Wow!' Sarah said. 'That's a really long list. Chance is going to need a miracle if he hopes to have all that in here by New Year's Eve.'

Molly frowned. 'It's longer than I expected. He doesn't have a thing apart from the Range cooker, a boiling water tap, which he's ridiculously proud of, a dishwasher, fridge-freezer, washing machine and tumble dryer. Oh, and one battered and paint-splattered chair. Even the mugs we use here are his mum's. But he does have built-in wardrobes in the bedrooms, so that's something, I suppose. Nevertheless, I think his girlfriend may be in for more of a surprise than he realises.'

'Yes. Especially when she discovers you and Miracle have been living with her boyfriend. I bet Chance hasn't told her about you.'

Molly tutted. 'Because there's nothing to tell. I'm just a friend helping out. Besides, I'll be leaving the day after she arrives. Oh, wait.

They will still let me and Miracle stay until New Year's Day, won't they?'

Sarah pulled a face, screwing up her mouth. 'I don't see why not. Isn't the plan for Chance and Jolene to move in here, anyway? So it'll just be you, Miracle, Vicky and Beauty at the other house for New Year's Eve night. Won't that be cosy?'

Molly hadn't thought about that. She'd tried not to think about Jolene at all, if she could help it.

'Nowhere near as cosy as Chance and Jolene will be,' she said, scowling. 'Wrapped in one another's arms in this gorgeous cottage, surrounded by snow, looking up from their sumptuous bed at a star-filled sky.'

Sarah nudged Molly's arm.

'Do I detect more than a hint of jealousy? Be careful of that, Molly.'

Molly sighed and looked Sarah directly in the eye.

'I will. At least I'll try. But Chance is just so bloody gorgeous. I've always had a crush on him. Ever since we were young. And I know I've hardly seen him over the years, but I'm feeling things for him that I know I shouldn't be feeling. And once or twice, I've seen him looking at me in a way that makes me think he might be feeling something too. There's definitely been 'a moment' once or twice. You know, when a guy looks at you as if he wants to

89

kiss you?'

Sarah nodded. 'I agree with you. I noticed that today. When you said we were going to be sitting on the kitchen counters, there was something in the way he looked at you that made me think he was having some sort of sexual fantasy. Of course, it may have been a fantasy about Jolene. Who knows? But it looked as though he had to drag his gaze from you.'

'Really?' Molly sat on her hands and sighed wistfully. 'I've been having a few fantasies of my own.'

'At least we can be sure that none of yours involve Jolene.'

Molly grinned. 'We can be absolutely sure of that. But I do need to keep reminding myself that she is Chance's girlfriend, and that she's the one who is going to be living in this house, not me.'

'Yeah. And you need to be careful about that too. Several of the things you bought today were things that you would like in your dream home. I'm not saying that Chance and Jolene won't like them too – in fact, I'm sure they will. You do have excellent taste. But don't forget, Chance is, effectively, a client. He's not your boyfriend.' Sarah flung her arm around Molly and hugged her tight. 'We need to find you a man of your own. I hate to say this, but even if Chance is interested in you, we can't ignore the fact that Jolene will be coming here to join him on New Year's Eve.'

'Or that he's going to propose to the bloody woman. And obviously she'll say yes.'

'He's going to what?' Sarah shrieked. 'Did you say he's planning to propose to Jolene on New Year's Eve?'

'Bugger!' Molly grabbed Sarah's hand in hers. 'That was supposed to be a secret. I promised Chance I wouldn't say a word. Oh God, I'm a horrible person and a really bad friend. Please don't say anything. Not even to Terry. Chance mustn't find out I've blabbed. He'll never forgive me.'

'Oh come on. It's not exactly a State secret. But it is bloody annoying.'

Molly eyed her friend. 'Annoying? Please don't tell me you like Chance as well.'

Sarah gave a roar of hysterical laughter. 'Of course not. I agree he's gorgeous, but I'm not interested in him in that way. I'm just annoyed that he's doing all this for Jolene, plus he's planning a romantic proposal on New Year's Eve and they've only been dating for about a year. They don't even live together in New York.'

'And your point is...?'

'My point is, Terry and I have been dating for four years this Christmas Eve, and living together for two, and yet there's absolutely no sign of a proposal, either now or in the future.

And that, Molly, is bloody annoying, let me tell you.'

Molly was surprised by Sarah's outburst. She had no idea her friend was feeling like that.

'Oh I see. Er. I don't know what to say. I could have a word with my brother, if you like.'

'No thank you!' Sarah snapped. 'I don't want him to be forced into proposing to me.'

'I wouldn't force him. Besides, I couldn't force Terry to do anything he didn't want to do. Although, according to Chance, I was able to do exactly that when we were young. Sorry. Going off on a tangent there. I'd just have a sisterly word with him. Make a suggestion. Give him some encouragement. Just like I did when he asked you out. You didn't mind me doing that. And I know you were glad I got you both beneath the mistletoe that Christmas Eve.'

Sarah smiled. 'Yes. I was glad about that. And I'm glad you encouraged him to ask me out. Well, to continue to ask me out, even though I rejected him so many times. But a marriage proposal is an entirely different thing. No one should propose to someone unless it's something they really want to do with every fibre of their being. They certainly shouldn't propose just because they think they should.'

'Chance!'

Molly spotted him hovering in the doorway, and she leapt off the kitchen counter.

Just how much of that conversation had he heard? By the look on his face, the tight line of his jaw, and the slight hint of red in his cheeks, he'd definitely heard some of it. And she suddenly realised that he probably thought they were discussing his plans to propose to Jolene. Which of course, they had been. But Molly didn't want him to know that.

'I've just come down to ask you to take a look at samples on the walls,' he said, avoiding eye contact with her.

'I'll come and look at them now. Be back in a minute, Sarah.'

'I'm coming too.' Sarah jumped down from the counter.

Molly tried to show her friend that she wanted to be alone with Chance for a moment, by gesturing with her hands and by the pleading expression on her face, but Sarah clearly didn't pick up on that.

'Chance!' Molly said again, only this time it was a plea. 'Please don't mention to Terry that you heard us talking about marriage proposals. Sarah was just telling me that, as they've been together for four years this Christmas Eve, she's hoping he might propose. I offered to give him a nudge in the right direction, but Sarah doesn't want that.'

'Oi!' Sarah glowered at Molly. 'Thanks for dropping me in it.'

Chance looked relieved. 'Oh I see. I

thought ... It doesn't matter what I thought.' He smiled at Sarah. 'Don't worry, Sarah. Your secret's safe with me. I won't say a word to Terry. I promise.'

'Thanks.' Sarah was still scowling at Molly.

'Sorry, Sarah.' Molly linked arms with her. 'But I had to say something, didn't I?'

'Oh yes. And I might have to say something too, if Terry gets to hear about this.'

Molly gave Sarah another pleading look and eventually Sarah smiled as they followed Chance upstairs.

Thirteen

Saturday had been the perfect day in Molly's estimation: shopping with Sarah in the morning, spending the afternoon at the cottage writing lists, and going over them that evening with Chance, Sarah and Terry while eating fish and chips that Chance and Terry had bought from the nearby chippy in Piemaker's Place. The bottle of Prosecco for her and Sarah and beers for themselves had added the final touch.

Afterwards, Terry and Sarah had gone home, and a short time later, Molly and Chance had walked back to his mum's, leaving Chance's car at the cottage because he'd been drinking. He'd offered to pay for a cab but Molly had laughed.

'It's a ten-minute walk at most, Chance. We don't need a cab.'

'But have you looked at the weather?'

He pointed up at the glass roof of the kitchen extension which was covered in a thick layer of snow.

'Which means we'd have to wait for ages for a cab as half of them are probably stuck in snowdrifts and the rest of them have no doubt listened to the forecast and stayed at home. We'll be fine.'

'I could take a chance and drive. I've only had a couple of beers.'

'No. There's no point in taking unnecessary risks. Besides, the police will be out in force tonight despite the snow. It's the last Saturday before Christmas and they've stepped up their 'don't drink and drive' campaign. Let's just walk.'

They'd hardly said a word to one another once they'd left the cottage. It seemed Molly wasn't the only one with a few things on her mind.

The air was bitterly cold and it took her breath away at first, but as they crunched through the snow in virtual silence, save for the occasional swishing noise as a car passed by on the gritted, partly slush-covered road, she grew accustomed to the freezing temperature.

The cottage was only around the corner from Vicky's, comparatively speaking, but in the deep snow, it took them about five minutes to reach the end of Wishing Well Lane – and that was quite a long time to be silent. At least it was for Molly.

'I hope you'll tell me if any of the things I bought today aren't to your taste. Or to

Jolene's. I can take any, or all of them, back. I'd rather know. And you won't hurt my feelings, I promise. Not that my feelings come into this. You're effectively a client and this is a professional relationship, even though we happen to be friends.'

He gave her a curious look and a wan smile, but after a second or two, he brightened and beamed at her.

'No. No, Molly. I loved everything you bought. Everything. I couldn't have chosen better myself.'

Molly grinned. 'Well, that was the whole point, wasn't it? You couldn't choose for yourself. That's why you asked me to help.'

'Good point. What I meant was that I want everything you bought, in my home. All of it. I can honestly say there wasn't one thing I didn't like. Not one.'

'Okay. That's a bit too much praise.' She grinned at him some more. 'But if, going forward, you don't like something, or you think your girlfriend won't, please just tell me straight away.'

He nodded. 'Okay. I will. But I don't think that'll happen. I can see why your design business is such a huge success. You really do have the ability to put together the perfect home. A dream home. I feel entirely safe in your hands. I mean, I feel my cottage is entirely safe in your hands. From an interior-design point of view.'

'I understand.' They took a short cut across a snow-covered grassy area that sat along the middle of the next road. 'I hope Miracle hasn't driven your mum crazy. Or wrecked the place. I feel a bit guilty for leaving him with her all day.'

'No need to. She offered. She loves dogs and she loves to feel needed. Believe me, you rescuing Miracle and coming to stay with us is probably the best thing that could've happened this Christmas.'

'Really?' Molly doubted that. 'I wish Miracle thought so. He's been sadly lacking in his appreciation.' She laughed softly. 'Not that I expected him to send me a Thank You card, or buy me a present or anything, but you know. It might be nice if he could stop causing havoc wherever he goes. Or at least refrain from peeing on people's Christmas trees.'

Chance threw her a look and laughed too. 'It was really good of you to stop and take him in. Not everyone would've done that.'

'Believe me, if I'd known there was no room at the inn, or anywhere else, I'd have left him where he was. The last thing I needed was a crazy dog.'

'No, you wouldn't. You're far too nice a person.'

A warm, fuzzy feeling was trickling through her and the way Chance was looking at her was making her go weak at the knees.

'What's Jolene like? Do you have a photo of her on you?'

'Jolene?' He said her name as if he'd forgotten who she was. 'Er. No. I'm not the sort of guy who carries photos in his wallet. I'm not the sort of guy who carries a wallet, so perhaps that's why.'

'Where d'you keep your money?'

He sniggered. 'That sounded as if you were going to mug me. I keep it in my pocket. I think I've got about eighty pounds and one bank card in there at the moment. And my phone.'

'That's almost worth mugging you for.'

'I'd like to see you try.'

'Believe me, I could take you in my sleep.'

'Oh yeah.'

'Yeah.'

They glanced at one another and sniggered.

'What about on your phone? Surely you've got a photo of her in your gallery? Or saved on the cloud or whatever.'

He shrugged. 'Nope.'

'What? Not one photo? Not even of the two of you together, having fun. Or on holiday or something? Or at a party? Everyone's got photos like that.'

He shook his head. 'Not me. I'm not really the kind of guy who takes random photos.'

'Random? Taking photos of you and your

girlfriend is hardly random. Are you human?'

'Superhuman.'

'Yeah, right. In your dreams. And I bet I could still take you.'

'Not in a million years.'

They grinned at one another, looked away and walked on. But after a few steps, Molly stuck out her right foot and tripped him up.

Falling, he reached out and grabbed her, managed to get his balance, but as laughter filled his eyes, he pulled her down with him onto the deep blanket of snow.

They rolled around play-fighting while she went for his jeans pocket, missed, and her hand caught him somewhere far more personal instead.

They both stopped laughing and looked at one another, Molly half on top of him, and his left hand tantalisingly close to her breast.

'Sorry,' she mumbled, blushing profusely as heat spread over her.

'No problem,' he replied, moving his hand a fraction closer to her breast before whipping it away and pushing himself – and Molly, to a sitting position.

She thought her head might explode. She had wanted so much for him to touch her breast. To caress her. To kiss her. And she'd had to tell herself not to leave her hand on his crotch.

'Okay,' she said, jumping to her feet. 'That

was fun. But now I think it's time we went home. Do you need help getting up? I know you're so much older than me.'

'Watch it,' he said, standing in one fluid move.

They walked on in silence once again, each smiling shyly when caught in the process of a surreptitious glance at the other. Molly was relieved when they reached Vicky's door ... until she spotted the huge bunch of mistletoe hanging in the porch. That hadn't been there this morning.

Chance stopped in his tracks a few feet from the porch and glanced around as if he were lost.

'Er. I think I dropped my phone in the snow just now. You go in without me. I'll only be a second.'

He dashed off before she had a chance to respond but she knew he was lying. He'd obviously seen the mistletoe too and had made that up to avoid a potentially embarrassing situation for them both.

Was that because he didn't want to kiss her?

Or because he did want to but knew he shouldn't?

He did, after all, have a soon-to-be fiancée.

But surely a kiss under the mistletoe wouldn't do any harm? And it wouldn't be cheating. It was simply tradition.

Except Molly knew that wasn't true.

It might do a lot of harm. And if Chance was feeling half of what she was, it would definitely be cheating, and might lead to so much more.

She must make a mental note. Mistletoe must be avoided at all costs. She must use the back door from now on.

Fourteen

Sunday morning brought pale lemon sunshine in through the chinks of the purple curtains in the guest room Molly occupied.

In spite of the fact that she loved snow, she was pleased to see the sun this morning. Today was the Sunday Christmas Market in Easterhill and Molly had promised to help Sarah man her stall.

Not that it would have mattered that much if the snow had continued. The Christmas Market was under cover as it was held in the middle of the shopping centre arcade. Molly had joked that if it had been outside, Sarah would've been on her own. But they both knew that wasn't true. Molly would happily stand in wind, rain or snow to help her friend. Well, maybe not happily, but she'd do it.

The only problem was, these plans had been made prior to Miracle entering Molly's life.

Over fish and chips last night, Sarah had

mentioned the market stall, and Molly had explained the situation to Chance.

'Not a problem,' he had said. 'Either Mum or I'll take care of Miracle for the day.'

'I can't ask either of you to do that,' Molly had said. 'You both took turns in looking after him today.'

'You didn't ask. I offered,' Chance had replied.

'Aren't you forgetting he tried to drown you?'

Chance had grinned. 'I'll have an opportunity to get my own back tomorrow.'

Molly had decided not to argue. She'd find a way to repay Chance and Vicky for their kindness.

This morning she hoped Chance was still in the same frame of mind, although there was no reason why he wouldn't be.

When they'd got in last night – Molly, a few minutes before Chance – Vicky was sitting in her loveseat beside a roaring fire, with Beauty snuggled on her lap. Miracle had draped himself along the back of the seat and his head was resting on Vicky's shoulder. She was reading out loud and it really looked as if Miracle and Beauty were listening intently to the story. All three of them were wearing Santa hats, and neither dog seemed bothered. It was such an adorable scene that Molly had taken a photo.

The strange thing was, in that split second, Molly had remembered that Miracle was a stray. And it hit her in her gut so hard that for a moment, she felt physically sick. Miracle didn't belong to her. She was only looking after him for Christmas. When the holidays were over, she'd be going back to Bristol and Asher would, hopefully, have found a place in a shelter for the dog.

But why did that bother her? He'd been nothing but trouble.

Except he wasn't. Not really. He was just a lost dog who needed love as much as anyone else. And right at that moment, Molly knew it would break her heart to know that she was the one who would be taking that love away from him.

But she couldn't take him on. She would have to leave him alone in her apartment for most of the day while she was at the homes of clients, or sourcing merchandise for them, and that wasn't fair to anyone.

Vicky couldn't adopt him either. Molly knew that, what with her upcoming operation and all the ongoing treatment that would entail. Chance would be looking after Beauty as it was. Well, Chance and Jolene, who would, by then, be Chance's fiancée. And Chance wouldn't take Miracle on. She couldn't expect him to. He had already told her that once the holidays were over and they had the results of

Vicky's operation, he'd need to start up a building firm in Easterhill, from scratch. He'd already agreed a sale of his building firm in the States so he would have the money from that to tide him over, but the cottage and all the work he'd done on that must've cost a small fortune and eaten into his savings. Not to mention the money he'd be spending on the interior.

When Molly had gone to bed on Saturday night, she'd been just as upset at the thought of losing Miracle as she was about losing Chance.

But today was another day. And the sunshine brought light and hope and a promise of better things to come.

It also brought dappled rays of sunlight onto the bed and Miracle chased the beams as if they were sticks.

Molly hugged him tight and he licked her face.

'We'll find a way, Miracle. I don't know how yet, but you're not going to a shelter if I can help it. Now let's get up and go for a walk in the sunshine.'

She would shower when they got back. The Christmas Market didn't open until eleven and although she and Sarah would need about an hour to pack the car, unload it at the shopping centre and set up the stall, there was plenty of time.

She went downstairs to find that no one else was up yet. She let Miracle out into the garden for a pee while she made Vicky and Chance some coffee. Yesterday, they'd brought her coffee in bed, so this was her opportunity to repay them. Although that hadn't turned out well for her, so she'd better make sure Miracle remained outside.

She asked the Smart Speaker to play some cheery Christmas music and she also asked for the weather for the day.

'Playing cheery Christmas music,' the speaker replied, and 'I Wish It Could Be Christmas Every Day' by Wizzard blared out.

'The old classics, I see,' Molly said, rolling her eyes even though she was alone in the kitchen.

'The weather for today is some sunshine mixed with cloud and a light, chilly breeze. Heavy snow is forecast later.'

'Excellent! Thank you.'

She made coffee and went upstairs humming the song she'd heard as she tapped on Vicky's door.

'Come in,' Vicky said, sounding sleepy.

'Did I wake you? Sorry.' Molly popped her head around the door. 'I've brought some coffee. Would you like me to let Beauty out for a pee?'

Vicky smiled and sat up in bed. 'Thank you, sweetheart. That's very kind. Yes please. I think I stayed up too late last night chatting with Chance.' She was giving Molly a curious smile.

'We had a very interesting talk.'

'That's good.' Molly wanted to ask what it was about but she knew she couldn't. She set the mug down on the bedside table and called Beauty to her. 'You can go back to sleep if you like. I'll take the dogs for a walk and then I'll make breakfast.'

'But you're helping Sarah at the Christmas Market, aren't you?'

'Yes. But not until later. There's plenty of time.'

'I might just have a few minutes more in that case,' Vicky said, sliding back down beneath the duvet. 'Thank you for the coffee.'

'It's a pleasure.'

Molly left the room and Beauty followed at her heels.

'Sit, Beauty,' she said, tapping on Chance's door.

She heard him say 'Come in' and she opened the door and walked inside.

But she got the shock of her life.

Chance was standing in the middle of his room, stark naked, looking as surprised as she was.

'You're naked!' she shrieked, unable to stop her eyes from scanning every inch of him. And there was a lot to scan. From his dripping wet hair to his broad shoulders; his firm chest and his six-pack; his manly hips, strong thighs and long legs. And everything in between.

Every part of him was perfect. Every. Single. Inch.'

'What the hell? Yes. I'm naked. And I'd appreciate it if you wouldn't stare at me as if you've never seen a naked man before.'

He turned and grabbed a towel and Molly admired his perfect bottom.

She'd seen a naked man before – quite a few, in fact – but never one who looked as good as Chance.

'Molly!' he snapped, wrapping the towel around his waist. 'You're spilling coffee all over the floor.'

'What? Oh God. Sorry.' She righted the mug but there was hardly any coffee left in it. 'But don't yell at me. You told me to come in.'

'No I didn't. I said, 'Coming'. As in, 'Wait outside. I'm coming to the door.'

'Oh. It didn't sound like that. Next time tell me to wait and then tell me you're coming.'

He raised his brows and a cheeky, sexy grin swept over his mouth. 'Are we still talking about the same thing?'

'What? Eew!'

She banged the virtually empty mug on the top of a chest of drawers and turned and walked away.

'Thanks for the coffee,' he called after her.

She could hear that he was laughing. But she'd also seen him blush when she'd first walked in.

If only she'd had her phone. She would've loved to have a photo of Chance in the buff. Although, in truth, she'd been far too shocked and embarrassed to have even considered taking a photo.

Fifteen

Sarah couldn't believe it when Molly gave her a blow-by-blow account at the Christmas Market later that morning.

'I think you heard exactly what he said but you pretended you misheard him so that you could see him naked.'

'And how would I have known he was naked? I swear to you, I was sure he told me to come in. Anyway, we haven't mentioned it since. I took the dogs out. Which nearly killed me, I might add. I should've bought a sled and they could've pulled me along on that in the snow. When I returned, Chance was already making breakfast and Vicky had just come down. He gave me a few odd looks across the table while we ate, but other than saying he'd take the dogs with him so that his mum could rest some more today, we hardly spoke at all.'

'So are you more besotted with him now you've seen all his bits, or less impressed than before?'

'Oh more. Much more. He's got some very impressive bits.'

They giggled like school girls while they set up the stall and were still giggling about it at the end of the day. Molly could hardly think of anything other than Chance standing naked before her.

Even the large number of customers she served throughout the day didn't distract her thoughts for long. And neither did listening to the carol singers who walked around the market dressed in Victorian finery, belting out several of Molly's favourite carols.

The arrival of Father Christmas on his sleigh which was pulled by a team of reindeer did take her mind off Chance for about five minutes, but when Santa asked her what she wanted for Christmas, Chance popped straight back into her head.

She'd looked around the other stalls and made a few purchases, both for herself and for the cottage, and that made her think, not just of Chance but also of his girlfriend.

'Have you ever seen a photo of Jolene?' Molly asked as she and Sarah packed up the few items they hadn't sold.

'No. Never. I'm not sure if Terry has but he hasn't mentioned it to me.'

'Don't you think that's odd? He doesn't even have a photo of her. At least he doesn't carry one around with him. Not even on his phone. You'd think he would, wouldn't you? Especially as they're thousands of miles apart.'

'Perhaps they videocall one another a lot.'

'Maybe. But still. You've got a photo of Terry on your phone, haven't you? And I know you've got one in your purse because you've shown it to me, several times in fact, usually when you're drunk. And I also know he's got several of you, and he does carry a wallet and there's one of you in that.'

'What's the big deal? Surely it's a good sign as far as you're concerned?'

'Why?'

'Because perhaps he's not as madly in love with Jolene as you think he is.'

'He's madly in love enough to be planning a romantic proposal on New Year's Eve.'

'Oh yeah. I forgot about that. Which reminds me.' Sarah thumped Molly's arm. 'Next time you break a promise, don't drag me into your lies to cover it up, okay?'

'Don't be such a grouch. I know you're not really mad because I can see your mouth twitching. But if it makes you happy, I promise I won't involve you next time.'

'And you promise me you haven't – and won't – say anything to Terry about what I said.'

'Scouts' honour.'

'That fills me with confidence. Are you going to take the things you bought here today to the cottage this evening?'

'I said I'd pop in, so yeah. Will you drop me off on the way home?'

'Of course. But just a friendly word of warning. If Chance tells you he's 'coming' when you knock on the door, wait for a minute or two before you burst in.'

'Oh very funny. He'll hardly be naked in the cottage, will he?'

'With Chance, anything's possible, I think.'

'If only that were true.'

They finished packing the stall away and climbed into Sarah's battered Land Rover.

'I think you should get Terry to buy you a new car rather than an engagement ring. This thing's on its last legs. Or should that be, last wheels?'

'I can buy my own car, thank you very much. I happen to love this old Land Rover, that's all. It has a lot of happy memories for me.'

'I get that. I loved Dad's old Land Rover. That had lots of happy memories for us. Terry and I were heartbroken when Dad sold it. And then, just a few months later, he and Mum were dead.' Molly let out a sigh. 'Life's strange, isn't it? I still miss them. We both do.'

'I know. You probably always will. It was a tragedy that they died so young.'

'At least they were together. And they were doing something they both loved. Apparently planes are still one of the safest forms of transport, or so the experts say. You stand more chance of being killed in a car crash than a plane crash.'

Sarah threw her a quelling look. 'Thanks for that. But talking of planes. Did you hear that more bad weather's coming? Heavy snow's expected tonight and some say we may have blizzard conditions. They're already saying they may have to close the airports and ground flights. If that continues over the holidays, Jolene might not make it here for New Year's Eve.'

'That'd be great, wouldn't it? Although not so great for everyone else trying to get to see their loved ones. And it would only delay the inevitable. If Chance doesn't propose on New Year's Eve, he'll propose at some stage afterwards. I hope Jolene realises how lucky she is to have a man like Chance. Ooh! I love this song. Turn it up, please.'

George Michael's 'Last Christmas' blasted out over the radio and Molly and Sarah sang along.

Molly was still singing it when Sarah dropped her off outside Wishing Well Cottage and Chance smiled at her when he opened the door.

'That's one of my favourite Christmas songs,' he said, stepping aside to let her in.

'You old romantic. I wouldn't have put you

down as a George Michael fan.'

'Not so much of the old. I'm only four years older than you. And I like a lot of different artistes, I'll have you know.'

'Noted. So how are you getting on here? And where is Miracle?'

She glanced along the hall and walked towards the sitting room.

'With Mum and Beauty, snuggled up in front of the fire, no doubt.'

'I feel really guilty getting your mum to look after him so much. She's spent more time with him than I have.'

Chance smiled. 'Don't feel guilty. I told you, Mum loves to feel needed. She's enjoying looking after Miracle. And two dogs are almost the same as one.'

'Really? Remind me again why you went for a swim. And why Sarah and Terry's tree isn't the shape it once was. And why they had to replace some presents. And a ham.'

'Okay. I'll admit Miracle is a bit of a handful, but he's different with Mum. You saw him last night. She said he'd been as good as gold. And all three of her trees are still standing. He hasn't touched them. It's as if he knows he's onto a good thing with Mum and he doesn't want to ruin it.'

'But it will be ruined, won't it?'

Molly slumped against the wall of the sitting room.

'Will it? Why?'

She met his look and held it for a moment but as tears suddenly welled up in her eyes, she let her head droop down.

'Because I'll be going back to Bristol and your mum's going into hospital and Miracle will have to go to a shelter. Assuming Asher can find one to take him in.'

'Hey.' Chance reached out and took her arm in his hand, gently easing her towards him. 'Don't get upset.' He placed his other hand on her other arm and held her a few inches away from him. 'Look at me, Molly. Please look at me.'

She slowly raised her eyes to his face. 'I … I know it's silly, and I've only had him since Friday, and he's spent more time with you and your mum than he has with me, but the thing is, I can't bear the thought of him not having a home to go to. I know I told Asher I'd take him just for Christmas, but he deserves a warm and loving home as much as anyone.'

'It's not silly at all. I like the little guy too. He sort of grows on you without you realising. He's grown on Mum as well. I don't know what the future holds, Molly, but I can promise you one thing. If you can't take him, which I don't suppose you can what with your business and everything, then either Mum or I will make sure he has a home. We won't let him go to a shelter. One of us will adopt him. Or we'll find someone else who will.'

'Really? You mean that? You're not just saying that to make me feel better?'

'I mean it and I'm not just saying it. I promise you. I'll be looking after Beauty. I can look after Miracle too. Don't worry about it. We'll work something out.'

'Oh Chance! You're the best. You truly are. Thank you! You don't know how much this means to me. Oh wait. What about your girlfriend?'

Chance stiffened. 'What about her?'

'She might not want another dog. She might be cross with you. Have you asked her?'

He shook his head and sighed softly. 'No. I haven't. But Jolene won't mind. She's ... very easy going.'

'Oh. I see.'

'Don't sound so disappointed. That's a good thing.'

'Yes. Yes, of course it is. That must be nice.'

'It is nice.'

'Yes. I can imagine.'

Molly coughed to clear her throat and edged away from Chance, who let his hands slide from her arms. She swiped the tears from her eyes and coughed again.

'Thank you, Chance. I really mean that. But if it turns out that Jolene doesn't want Miracle, I'll understand.'

'Whatever happens, Molly, I made a

promise and I intend to keep it. Miracle won't go to a shelter. We'll sort something out. Trust me on that.'

'I do trust you, Chance.' She needed to change the subject. She was getting far too emotional. And the way Chance had held her just now and looked into her eyes had sent feelings rushing through her that threatened to make her do something stupid. Like kiss him or something. And she definitely couldn't do that. 'Right. Sorry. I'm being silly and we've still got a lot to do here.' She moved farther away. 'Oh. I bought a couple of things from the Christmas Market. What do you think of these?'

She held up a pair of wrought iron, bedside lamps. They were simple in design, just a swirl or two of jet-black metal, rising from a small, circular base and ending in one long stem which curved over to one side.

'They're beautiful, Molly.'

'They're for your bedroom.'

He nodded. 'Yes. I thought they were.'

'Okay. Let's discuss furniture for in here. Have you decided which of the sofas you like best from the ones I suggested? You'll need to order them soon, or they'll never be here in time for New Year's Eve. Not even from the local stores.'

'Molly? Are you okay?' He was looking at her with genuine concern.

'Yes. I'm fine. Absolutely great. But I keep

forgetting, I'm here to work. We had a deal and you've certainly kept up your side of it. I need to keep up mine. So. Which sofa, or sofas, have you chosen?'

'You've kept up your end of it too. You'll get no complaints from me. But you're not just here to work, Molly. You're here because you're my friend. And you mean a lot to me. Your opinion means a lot to me.'

'Thanks. But time is ticking and it waits for no man. Or woman. Let's make a decision and get these sofas ordered. And while you're doing that. I'll go and make some tea. I'm gasping all of a sudden.'

Nothing more was said about providing Miracle with a home, nor about Jolene, and as the weather had taken a turn for the worse, they hadn't stayed at the cottage much longer.

Driving home, both were once again deep in their own thoughts and although Molly tried to make conversation about how heavy the snow was becoming and how icy the roads were getting, Chance didn't seem to want to talk.

The drive took about four minutes, and yet again, Chance made an excuse to let Molly go indoors before him to avoid them being under that damn mistletoe together. This time he said he needed something from his boot and he'd be inside in a second.

Molly went in without him and saw that Vicky was fast asleep on the loveseat and so were both of the dogs.

'I'll make dinner,' Molly offered, when Chance came in a few minutes later, and he didn't argue with that.

She made pasta with mushrooms, walnuts and blue cheese, having checked with both Vicky and Chance that they liked the sound of that.

Afterwards, with varying amounts of input from both Molly and his mum, Chance finally made several decisions about sofas and other furniture and placed a number of orders to be delivered over the coming days and between the Christmas break and New Year. Most of the items were from local stores, and were being delivered from stock, so at least the waiting times were short.

Molly went to bed, again before Chance and his mum. It had been yet another strange day and her feelings for Chance were growing deeper.

She would have to be careful of that.

But the way he'd looked at her when she'd got upset about Miracle, made her think she wasn't the only one who needed to take care.

Sixteen

Monday morning brought the heaviest snowfall the UK had seen in some time. It wasn't exactly the blizzard some had predicted; there wasn't any wind, but thick snow had fallen throughout the night and by morning there were several inches covering the ground.

Even the dogs showed their surprise. Beauty, by stopping in her tracks and needing to be coaxed into going outside; Miracle, by diving head first into the deep drift and completely disappearing, only to resurface, nose first, a few feet away from the house, like the periscope of a submarine

Chance had been the first one up, but only by a few seconds, and Molly and Vicky shrieked with delight when they saw the amount of snow outside.

'It might look beautiful,' Chance said, as he made coffee, 'but it's going to mean delays with the cottage, which is a nuisance to say the least. None of the things we ordered last night will make it through in this.'

'We both warned you that you were leaving things very late, darling,' Vicky said, somewhat unhelpfully.

'Thanks, Mum.' Chance frowned at her.

'Don't give me that look.' She grinned at him. 'You've only got yourself to blame.'

'Nothing is arriving until Wednesday,' Molly said. 'Conditions may be better by then. I can't remember the last time we had a white Christmas, so it'll probably melt in a day or so and life will be back to normal.'

'I admire your optimism,' Chance said, feeling life, at least for him, would never be normal again.

He'd hardly got any sleep last night. All he had thought about was how badly he'd wanted to kiss Molly as he'd tried to reassure her about Miracle. He'd managed to keep her at arm's length, but the urge to pull her to him had been so strong and he wasn't sure how much longer he could fight the intense attraction he was feeling.

He had never cheated on anyone in his life and this definitely wasn't the time to start. He'd bought a ring, for God's sake and was planning to propose to Jolene on New Year's Eve, but whenever he tried to picture it, the only person he was able to visualise standing before him as he got down on one knee in the cottage, was Molly, not Jolene.

It was only because he was spending so much time with Molly. Wasn't it? And because he and Jolene were thousands of miles apart. They video-called one another every day but that wasn't the same.

And that wasn't true. It was Jolene who made all the calls. Chance kept forgetting.

But it was difficult to remember he had to call his girlfriend when he had so much else on his mind. Like getting the cottage finished without Jolene finding out what he was planning. And being anxious about a stray dog that had come into his life. And worrying about his mum even though she seemed happier than she had been in a long, long time.

And then there was the time difference. Remembering that New York was five hours behind was a bit of a pain, especially at ten o'clock at night when all he wanted to do was have a shower, clean his teeth and go to bed.

But even that wasn't true. Since Friday, all he thought about at ten o'clock each night was Molly sleeping in the bed just two doors away from his room.

How had he let this happen? How had he become so involved with Molly? And he was involved, whether he liked it or not.

I mean Jesus Christ, he'd even offered to adopt Miracle, and the last thing he needed was some crazy, out of control dog nipping at his heels.

But the truth was, he was falling in love with the damn dog almost as fast as he was falling in love with Molly.

Shit! Falling in love with Molly? How could that be the case? He'd known her for most of his life. Why in hell would he be falling in love with her now? Surely it was just lust? Or because of the situation? Surely this couldn't be real?

No. It was just because they were doing up the cottage. It felt as if they were planning their home together and they weren't. Wishing Well Cottage wasn't Molly's home and it never would be.

So why did he see her image in every room whenever he walked into it? Or hear her laughter in the wind outside?

Because he was clearly losing his mind. That's why.

He was not falling in love with Molly Ford.

He wasn't.

He couldn't be.

It wasn't possible.

It was because of the season.

There was magic in the air.

At least there was whenever Molly was nearby.

Or even in his thoughts.

Which she seemed to be all the time.

Nope. He wasn't falling in love with Molly. It was just because it was Christmas. And

Christmas was the time to be with those you loved.

Except he didn't love Molly. He loved Jolene. He needed to remind himself of that. And there was no better time to start than the present.

In spite of the time difference, he would video-call Jolene.

He told his mum and Molly that he was going to take a shower, and he skulked off to his room.

'Chance? Honey, is that you? What time is it? Has something bad happened?'

Jolene looked beautiful. Stunningly so. Especially in that low-cut, see-through negligee.

And yet he'd been far more turned on when he'd seen Molly in her polar bear PJs and had glimpsed her breast for the merest second.

'Sorry. I shouldn't have called. It must be about three in the morning there. Nothing's wrong. Everything's fine. I just … I just wanted to hear your voice, that's all.'

'Aww, honey. That's so sweet. I miss you too.'

'It's snowing heavily here. What's it's like in New York?'

'Snowing. And it's bad. There hasn't been snowfall like this for an age.'

'Same here. The authorities are advising people not to travel unless it's an emergency.'

She peered at the screen. 'Are you telling me I shouldn't come over?'

'What? No. No, I'm not saying anything of the sort. Of course you should come over. You must. In fact the sooner you're here the better. I need you here.'

'Honey! You know what? I think that's the nicest thing you've ever said.'

'The nicest thing? Oh come on. I've said nicer things than that.'

Hadn't he? They'd dated for almost a year. He must've done.

She shook her head. Her laughter didn't sound as cheery as Molly's laugh.

'Na-uh.' She suddenly grew serious. 'You've never even said you love me.'

Chance swallowed. Hard. Tiny beads of sweat prickled his skin. His heart beat a little quicker.

He'd never said he loved her? Could that be right? Was that true?

He took a second to think and realised Jolene was right. He hadn't said those words.

Not once.

And yet he was planning to propose to her in ten days' time.

Now would be a good time to say it.

'You've never said you loved me either.'

She sighed and sadness filled her eyes.

'I have, honey. More than once. You've just never said it back.'

'Really? Shit! I'm sorry. Well, I'm saying it now.'

Except he wasn't. And both he and Jolene knew that.

Why couldn't he simply say it? It wasn't complicated. It wasn't a matter of life or death.

Except it sort of, was.

'I love you too, honey. I can't wait to see you on New Year's Eve. And to meet your mom. I hope she's looking forward to meeting me.'

'Er. Yes. Yes she is. I'd better go because I promised I'd make breakfast. Sorry I woke you up. Speak soon. Sleep well.'

He closed his laptop with a groan and banged his head on it.

'Speak soon. Sleep well.' What kind of boyfriend was he? All Jolene wanted to hear were three little words. Maybe four. 'I. Love. You. Jolene.' There. He'd said it. Only not to her.

And why did it feel as if he'd just told the biggest lie ever?

He'd have to do some serious thinking. But not right now. His mum was calling him and he could hear Molly in the background, laughing.

Shortly after breakfast, the snowfall turned into a full-blown blizzard. News reports said flights were being grounded and several UK airports closed. Numerous roads across the country were blocked and entire villages cut off. This was the worst blizzard in living memory and people were predicting a miserable Christmas for some. There were power cuts in certain parts, but thankfully not in Easterhill or anywhere in the county. Wales was hit badly and so were parts of Scotland and the Midlands; the South of England came off better than most.

Molly, Vicky and Chance stayed indoors for most of Monday, only venturing out once to try to give the dogs some exercise. But trying to do that in over a foot of snow proved difficult and the dogs didn't seem to mind spending the day curled up in front of the fire.

Chance hadn't minded either, even though he still had so much to do at the cottage. But he could give himself one day off and it had been years since he had played Monopoly and all the other board games both Molly and his mum had suggested they play. It was actually a lot of fun.

They'd eaten pizza that the three of them had made from scratch. They'd also made mince pies, shortbread biscuits and a rather misshapen Yule Log. Molly baked some gingerbread men which she turned upside down and made to look like reindeers by drizzling various colours of icing on them. She used white icing on the legs to make them into antlers, and on the arms to make into the reindeer ears. She added two blobs of blue icing on the body to make eyes and used red in the centre for the nose. A black half circle on what was once the head of the man, made a mouth.

'They look amazing, Molly,' Chance said as he took two.

They tasted pretty amazing as well.

The three of them watched the news from time to time throughout the day where images of people trudging through the snow to get to where they needed to be, made Chance, Molly and Vicky grateful that they didn't need to be anywhere at all.

Molly had called Terry and Sarah a couple of times and both of them were staying in.

'Sarah's spending the day at her sewing machine,' Molly said when she rang off. 'Terry's taking a 'snow day' but Sarah's asked him to do some DIY around the house.'

Terry was an accountant so it wasn't as if a day off would be a major event, unlike all the police, firemen, doctors and nurses and other necessary services. Most of those did struggle to make it in, according to the news reports.

The local authority did what they could to clear the roads or at least make them passable, but they stated on the website that travelling anywhere other than a mile or so from your own front door, required determination, dedication ... and several tonnes of their grit. Once the gritting lorries could get out, that is.

Seventeen

The blizzard finally eased on Tuesday but snow continued to fall, on and off, all day.

Even so, Chance and Molly made it to the cottage, leaving Miracle with Vicky once again, and they both got quite a bit done.

Chance painted the sitting room a deep, dark bottle green. Molly had said it needed a bright, bold colour and the room suited the green perfectly. Or the green suited the room. It made the fireplace stand out, and brought out the warmth in the polished oak floorboards.

Together with the rich, ruby red sofas he'd ordered and a modern, patterned red, green and yellow rug that Molly had said she loved, it would look both classy and cosy. And once the fire was lit and the lights turned low, it would also be romantic.

There would be two chestnut brown leather armchairs either side of the fire, with tartan, pure wool throws to add more colour and to wrap up in if it was a particularly cold night. Some plain cushions in reds, greens and yellows and some patterned ones would add to the look even more. And Chance's books alone would fill the built-in bookcases each side of the fireplace and chimney breast.

He'd yet to choose a coffee table but he could pick one of those up locally.

The master bedroom was now navy blue and plaster pink, as per Molly's vision. The only things in that room so far were the two bedside lamps. He really needed to get a bed. And bedding. And curtains. And ... his mind drifted off again and as always, it was Molly he saw in that bed, not Jolene.

He really needed to get a grip.

He spent the rest of the day doing his very best to avoid being too close to Molly. If she came into a room, he made an excuse to leave it. If they were about to pass one another in either hall, he detoured into another room until she had gone.

He was very glad when Sarah and Terry turned up unexpectedly with lunch of pie and chips.

'I hope you've remembered what today is,' Sarah said, as they all sat on the sitting room floor and admired his paintwork.

'It's Tuesday,' Chance said.

'It's the annual Snowball Pie event,' Molly reminded him. 'And I think that when we've finished lunch, we should all go into the garden and practise.'

'Throwing snowballs?' Chance wasn't enamoured with the idea.

'Winning,' Molly said, giving him a hard stare but ruining the effect by grinning.

'Ah. Right. Okay then. If I must, I must.'

And half an hour later, all four of them were having a snowball fight. They started off in teams of two; girls against boys, but it soon ended up as everyone for themselves, although Chance seemed to be coming off the worst. But he couldn't remember a snowball fight ever being so much fun. In fact, he couldn't remember when he'd last had a snowball fight. Lately, he seemed to be doing and thinking and feeling a lot of things he hadn't done, or thought, or felt for a long time. And most of that was due to Molly.

So he was determined to do his best to make sure they won the annual Snowball Pie event that evening.

Eighteen

The garden of The Piemaker's Rest looked magical. The thick layer of snow glistened and reflected a kaleidoscope of colour from the myriad multi-coloured fairy lights hanging from the hedges, trees and posts surrounding the large open space of snow-covered grass. For the first time in years, the annual Snowball Pie would be using real snow, and no one seemed more delighted about that than Molly.

'Everyone, line up in teams of two,' Rupert, one of the pub's owners, said. 'For those of you newly joining us, one team member should collect a tinfoil baking tray which my lovely partner, Maud, is handing out. That's the 'pie'. The other team member must stand behind the Christmas ribbon we've laid out on the snow. If you cross the ribbon, you're out. Your challenge is to pick up and throw as many snowballs into the pie as possible in two minutes and the team with the most balls in their pie, wins. No pushing or shoving of other competitors is allowed, but after the competition winners are declared, snowball fights are encouraged. Good luck, folks.'

'And this year,' his partner Maud, added, 'because we've finally got real snow, we're adding an extra prize. In addition to the highly coveted keyrings, the winning team will get dinner for two in our superb, but admittedly bijou, restaurant.'

A loud 'Coooo!' went up from the crowd, followed by much laughter.

'Okay,' Molly said. 'We're going to win this, Chance.'

'I didn't realise you were so competitive. I thought you were joking the other day, but you really do want to win, don't you?'

'What's wrong with that?' She frowned at him.

Chance shook his head. 'Nothing. It's good to see someone so passionate about what they want. I'll try not to let you down. Am I throwing or catching?'

'Catching. I'm good at this.'

'I remember from our snowball fights of old. You always pummelled me and Terry. But don't you need to be gentle for this?'

'I can be gentle, Chance. Believe me.'

And yet another unwanted image popped into Chance's head. He coughed to clear his throat, turned to take a pie from Maud, and took up his position opposite Molly.

'Don't let your balls fall out,' one of the spectators shouted to the teams, and everyone cheered and whooped with laughter.

'Are you ready, teams?' Rupert shouted. 'You can pick up your first snowball when I ring my Christmas bells and you must stop as soon as I ring them again after two minutes. On your marks. Get set. Go!'

He rang the bunch of silver bells he was holding and the crowd roared with shouts of encouragement.

Molly was like a machine. She bent down and picked up two snowballs at once and threw them towards Chance. They landed in the pie with a soft splat, but they didn't fall apart.

Chance was impressed, until one snowball bounced off his nose. Although miraculously, that remained intact too and landed in the pie. He glanced at Sarah who stood close by. Her pie wasn't as full as his and Terry definitely wasn't as good at throwing snowballs as Molly. None of the competitors' pies were as full. They might actually win this thing. He was surprised at how much he wanted to. He hadn't realised he was that competitive.

Or did the prospect of a dinner for two have something to do with his sudden eagerness to win?

'Come on, Molly,' he yelled, beaming at her.

It wasn't long before they heard the bells,

and those who continued throwing were disqualified. That accounted for three teams, and some of the crowd good-naturedly pounded the losers with snowballs.

'Wait until we've declared the winners,' Rupert scolded them, but with a broad grin on his red face.

He and Maud inspected all the remaining pies and to Chance's delight, he and Molly were pronounced the 'Supreme Snowball Pie Makers of the Year'.

Molly ran to Chance and he caught her in his arms, spinning her around for a moment before letting her slide down the length of his body until her feet were set on the snowy ground. Their eyes were locked and their mouths were inches apart and Chance had to fight back the urge to kiss her. Thankfully for him, Terry came and slapped him on the back.

'The drinks are on you, mate. Well done, sis. We'll get your crowns from you next year.'

The crowns were paper hats and Molly and Chance were crowned and handed their keyrings with the fluffy snowmen attached.

'Who's going to look after the voucher for the romantic dinner?' Maud asked, winking at them.

Molly shot a look at Chance. 'Oh. Er. Why don't you take that? You can use it when your girlfriend arrives.'

Maud gave Chance a surprised look as she

handed it to him, and although he took it, he shook his head.

'No way, Molly. You earned this. Couldn't we have dinner together? As friends, of course. It doesn't have to be romantic.'

'I ... I suppose we could. Yes. That would be nice. Thank you.'

'No. *Thank* you. I had a really good time. And now I've got a crown, a keyring that may one day be a collector's item, a fluffy snowman and the prospect of a lovely dinner to look forward to. Not to mention that I've done my small bit to add to the coffers of a worthy charity. Does life get any better than this?'

Molly was giving him an odd look, as if she wasn't sure what to make of his comments.

'Are you being sarcastic again?'

'No. I'm serious. Although maybe I was being a little sarcastic about the keyring becoming a collector's item.'

She smiled at him now. 'You might be surprised. Come on. Let's go and buy my loser of a brother and his loser of a girlfriend some drinks. There's Christmas punch or mulled wine if you fancy either of those.'

'Be still my beating heart,' he said. 'And yes. That was sarcastic. I need a pint of beer.'

Nineteen

The snow finally stopped falling and by Wednesday morning, sunshine poured down from a bright, blue sky.

Another weather front was moving in, according to the forecasts, and was likely to bring more snow with blizzard conditions once again, probably by Christmas Eve, so it was definitely going to be a white Christmas.

But when the snow began to melt on Wednesday, Chance was relieved to say the least. His furniture might make it to the cottage, after all. Even if the respite might only be brief.

He took both dogs for a walk, leaving Molly and his mum at home, and returned in time for breakfast.

Vicky said she wanted to do some last-minute Christmas shopping, but due to the icy conditions on the pavements and the roads, Chance didn't want her to go alone. Before he had time to say he would take her, Molly had offered instead.

'If that's okay with you and your mum,' she said.

'I would love that.' Vicky sounded thrilled. 'If you're sure you don't mind, sweetheart.'

'Mind?' Molly laughed and grinned at Chance. 'I can't think of a better way to spend the day. Unless you need me at the cottage?'

'No,' he said, beaming at her. 'I'll be painting for most of the day. And praying that some of the furniture arrives. You would probably be in the way.' He winked at her and silently mouthed the words, 'Thank you.'

She smiled at him and nodded and he hoped she understood how much her offer had meant to him. He had never seen his mum so happy and it filled his heart with pleasure to see the pure joy written all over Vicky's face.

'Would you like us to get you anything while we're out?' Molly asked. 'Like a beautiful Christmas present for me, for example?'

She was clearly joking, but it made him think. Not only had he not yet bought a present for Molly, he hadn't bought any presents for his mum. Once the furniture arrived, he would have to sneak away and do some Christmas shopping of his own.

'Thanks. But I can buy a bar of chocolate anywhere.'

'Make sure it's milk chocolate, because I don't like dark. And it had better be a big bar.'

'It'll be big. You have my word on that. I might even stretch to two bars if you're really good.'

'I'm always good. In fact, I'm nothing short of an angel.'

'I agree with that,' Vicky said. 'You've definitely brought some light into our lives since you've been here.'

Molly blushed, and Chance felt something surge inside him, especially when he saw her glance at him beneath her lashes, the green flecks in her beautiful hazel eyes sparkling and an awkward smile creeping across those soft, pink lips.

'Thanks,' Molly said. 'But I think the truth is that I've brought you quite a lot of trouble and inconvenience. And I don't just mean in the shape of Miracle. The last thing you expected was to have me and a stray dog staying for the holidays.'

'Nonsense.' Vicky shot a look at Chance. 'Having you here and Miracle, of course, has been wonderful. And I'm sure my son agrees.'

'I do,' he said. 'I've loved having you here. You and your daft dog.' He coughed and turned away. 'But I'd better get on. There's still a lot to do. Have fun, you two. I'll take the dogs with me.'

'Move the Christmas tree,' Molly said. 'Just in case. Miracle hasn't caused havoc for a couple of days. He might need to let off some

141

steam.'

He wasn't the only one. Chance was feeling pretty hot under the collar himself right now.

Why did Molly always look so damn good?

Even in jeans, a Christmas themed sweater, her hair tied back in a ponytail and not a trace of make-up on her face, she managed to look as sexy as hell.

And for the umpteenth time, he told himself, that he must stop fantasising about making love with Molly Ford.

It was never going to happen.

The sooner he took that on board the better it would be.

For everyone.

Twenty

The following day was Christmas Eve and snow was falling again, as the forecasters had predicted.

Thankfully, most of Chance's furniture had arrived the day before, although he still didn't have a bed in any of the bedrooms. At this rate he would be sleeping on the floor.

'You can take the bed from your room,' Vicky offered. 'At least you'll have something to sleep on until your new beds arrive. But you'll need to hire a van or something to move it.'

'If it comes apart,' Molly said, 'it can go in the back of Sarah's Land Rover. There's plenty of room in there.'

'That's not a bad idea. And it's another problem solved. Thanks Mum. And thanks for the suggestion, Molly.'

'I'm here to help. So what's the plan for today? Any deliveries expected? Or anything I can do at the cottage?'

'Two deliveries. But I can deal with those.

And everything else is done, I think. Apart from giving the place a final clean and tidying up my tools, brushes and paint cans.'

'I can help with that.'

'So can I,' said Vicky. 'I haven't been much help so far. I'd like to do my bit on Christmas Eve. And as you said last night, darling, you need to do some last-minute Christmas shopping. Why don't you do that once the deliveries arrive, and leave me and Molly to do the clearing up?'

Molly nodded. 'That sounds like a plan. But why do men leave their Christmas shopping until the very last minute? I just don't get it.'

'Because we have other, more manly things to do,' Chance said, knowing he was playing with fire. 'And because we can buy chocolate bars at any time, even on Christmas Eve.'

'And perfume,' Molly said, looking thoughtful. 'Men always buy chocolates and perfume, don't they? Oh. And horrendous underwear that they think is sexy but their girlfriends usually don't.'

'Don't you like sexy underwear?'

He had a sudden vision of Molly wearing a sheer, black basque, along with black patent, thigh-length boots. He quickly dismissed the vision. What a cliché. He certainly wouldn't be buying her underwear. Sexy or otherwise.

'Of course I do. Just not usually the so-called sexy underwear that any of my boyfriends ever bought me. And no. Before you ask, I am not going into details.'

'And jewellery,' Vicky said. 'A lot of men buy jewellery.'

'So,' Chance said. 'Apart from the sexy underwear, that's basically everything on my shopping list.'

'Perhaps you need my help with that,' Molly said. 'As well as giving you the benefit of my interior designer talents, I'm happy to be your personal, Christmas shopper.'

He liked the sound of that.

'New plan,' Vicky said, smiling. 'Basically it's the same plan as earlier except that, once the deliveries have arrived, you and Molly should go shopping, I'll look after the dogs, and then all three of us can return to the cottage to do the cleaning. How about that?'

'And put up more decorations,' Molly added. 'So far there's only a tree. And to be completely honest, that still smells a little of Miracle's pee.'

'Didn't you say you won dinner for two at the pub?' Vicky asked. 'Why don't you do that tonight?'

'It's Christmas Eve, Mum,' Chance said, darting a look at Molly.

'I know it is, darling, but so what?'

'Well for one, they're probably fully booked, and for two, aren't we all going to spend it together? Or do you have plans with Sarah and Terry, Molly?'

'No. Terry told me weeks ago that he wanted a romantic Christmas Eve meal with Sarah, so I'd be spending the night on my own. I planned to have a long soak in the bath and a pampering session, a few Baileys and a bucket-load of chocolates and watch several hours of Christmas movies. That was before Miracle came into my life, of course.'

'Oh that sounds like heaven,' Vicky said. 'Minus the alcohol. I'd have hot chocolate instead. With whipped cream. And marshmallows. And grated chocolate. That's what I'm going to do. So even if the pub is booked, I'm afraid I'll need you two to go elsewhere for a few hours. You can come home at ten-thirty and we can watch a carol concert, or Christmas film, or open a present or two. But not before ten-thirty. Okay? And before you ask. The dogs are staying with me. They both need some pampering too.'

'Mum!' Chance sounded cross. 'That's not very polite to our guest.'

'Oh don't mind me,' Molly said, laughing. 'I can make myself scarce. I don't mind at all. I could still go round to Terry's. I'm sure he wouldn't mind. You can come too, if you want.'

He grinned. 'Thanks. I like the sound of the bath, the Baileys and the chocolates. The Christmas movies, not so much.'

Molly tutted. 'Obviously I'd forego the bath if you were there. And we don't have to watch Christmas movies, I suppose. But there is no way I'm sitting through a bunch of *Star Wars* films, so forget it if that's what you're thinking.'

He burst out laughing. 'I wasn't. But now you've mentioned it.' He rubbed his clean-shaven chin as if deep in thought. 'Seriously though. If we're going to be spending the evening together, we might as well see if we can go to the pub for dinner. Or somewhere nicer. I don't mind. It'll be my treat.'

'Somewhere nicer than The Piemaker's Rest! Does such a place exist?' Her voice dripped sarcasm. 'All joking aside, the pub sounds great to me. If we can get a table.'

'I'll call them now and ask. Do you have the number?'

Molly searched her bag for her phone. 'Mention my name. They know me well in there. And they know Sarah and Terry even better. I hope that's not where he's taking her tonight. That would be quite funny. Ask Maud or Rupert when you call. Wait. Why don't I do it?'

Before he had time to reply, she'd dialled the number and was smiling at him.

'Hi, Maud. It's Molly. Merry Christmas to you and Rupert. Listen, you know Chance and I won that dinner for two, do you happen to have a table free for tonight? We'll pay the extra as it's Christmas Eve. But has my brother booked a table? You can? Excellent. He hasn't. No. That's fine. We'll see you and Rupert at seven. And I already know I'll be having your turkey, port and cranberry pie with all the trimmings. Bye for now.'

'Turkey, port and cranberry pie?' Chance repeated. 'Not exactly cordon bleu.'

'Nope. Not one of your posh New York restaurants, but if you haven't eaten one of their pies, you haven't lived. Believe me, you'll love it.'

'That's settled then,' Vicky said, beaming. 'I think this may be one of the best Christmas Eve's yet. For all of us.'

Twenty-One

'Wow!' Chance said, as his gaze swept over Molly. 'You look fantastic.'

Molly hoped her cheeks weren't as pink and shiny as her new dress. The way Chance was smiling at her with that admiring look in his eyes was making her temperature rise and her mind imagine all sorts of things.

And the way he was dressed didn't help. Until this evening she'd only seen him in jeans, T-shirts or old shirts and jumpers. Now he wore a pair of expensive-looking, navy trousers, an equally classy, white shirt with one button undone at the neck, and a navy cashmere sweater with a surprisingly cheesy, Christmas motif of Father Christmas and his reindeer flying across a starry, moonlit night sky.

Yet he looked so sexy that when they walked into the pub restaurant and hung up their coats on the rack, after Molly had nipped to the ladies to change from her snow boots into a pair of strappy, silver sandals, she realised she wasn't the only girl there who was wishing he was her boyfriend.

'Thanks,' she said. 'You don't look bad yourself. Er. Do those stars light up?'

He grinned. Pressed one and said, 'Ta dah!'

All four stars and the moon twinkled at her.

'Nice. Bet you didn't get that off a stall in the old 'flea market'. She was referring to some stalls they'd seen that afternoon selling very cheap, and rather flimsy-looking, Christmas jumpers.

'Nope. But I did buy it today. I thought you'd appreciate my effort to get into the Christmas spirit, after nagging me earlier because I said I thought six huge bags of Christmas decorations were probably enough.'

Molly tutted and laughed. 'You can never have enough decorations. But I do appreciate it. It's perfect.'

'Thanks. I bet you didn't get that dress from the market either.'

Again, his eyes scanned her from head to toe and she was glad she'd changed her footwear.

'This old thing.' She blushed as she said it.

She knew she looked really good. She'd only bought the sequined satin halter- neck midi today, when Chance had said he needed thirty minutes on his own. She'd joked that he would need a lot longer than that to find her the perfect present to which he'd replied, 'You might be surprised', before looking a little awkward and embarrassed. They'd arranged to meet in The Cherry Topped Café in half an hour, and it had been Molly who had kept him waiting, not the other way around.

She hadn't been looking for a dress, but it had made her stop in her tracks as she'd walked past the store window. She hurried inside and tried it on and she didn't want to take it off.

It clung in all the right places and the sequins were so small you could hardly see them but they made the dress sparkle between pink and silver depending on how the light hit it.

The long slit that ran up the front of her left thigh wasn't just sexy, it made her feel taller, somehow. And because of the halter neck, she couldn't wear a bra. She couldn't get on with those strapless ones and besides, everyone told her how pert her breasts were. Some said they were her best feature.

Chance wasn't staring at them like some men did though, he was taking in all of her and it was pretty clear he liked what he saw.

'Molly Ford!' Rupert, the pub owner said, hurrying over to her as she and Chance waited to be seated. 'My, my. Don't you look a picture? Maud, sweetie. Have you seen our Molly? If you weren't the life of my life, sugarplum, this handsome young man might have competition for our Molly's heart.'

'Oh. We're not ... that is ... we're friends, Rupert. Just friends. But thank you for the compliment.'

Now she really was the colour of her dress, and Maud made things worse.

'Oh. My. Pickled. Onions! Don't you just look the bee's knees? In all the years we've known you, I don't think I've ever seen you look so beautiful. But that's what Love does.' She tapped Chance on the arm as Molly tried to explain, yet again that they were only friends. 'I hope you realise how lucky you are, young man. Our Molly's very special.'

'I know. Believe me,' Chance said, smiling at Molly as if he agreed with everything Rupert and Maud had said.

Molly stared at him, open-mouthed, for at least three seconds.

'We've saved 'The Lover's Nook' just for you two,' Rupert said, which made Molly colour-up even more, and Chance look a little unsure of what to say.

'I'm so sorry about all that,' Molly said, as soon as they were seated and Rupert and Maud had gone about their business.

'That's okay. It wasn't your fault.'

Now, his gaze darted everywhere other than at her.

'It's only because they saw us together at

the Snowball Pie event, and because tonight's Christmas Eve and we've both got a bit dressed up for the occasion, they've put two and two together and made fifty. But I always dress up if I go out on Christmas Eve. And they always make a big thing of it if I happen to come in here.'

That last part wasn't quite true, but he wouldn't know that.

And she did dress up if she was going out, but tonight she'd made an extra special effort.

He definitely didn't need to know that.

Chance relaxed slightly and smiled.

'Shall we have champagne? It is Christmas Eve, after all.'

'Oooh yes. I love champagne. But we're going halves on the bill, okay? Our prize covers dinner for two with wine, but tonight they have a special Christmas menu and it's more expensive than usual.'

'That's fine. But we're not splitting the bill. Don't argue.'

'This isn't a date, Chance. I'm not having you pay for me.'

His jaw locked and his eyes flashed as if she'd just slapped his face.

'I'm well aware it's not a date, Molly. You don't have to remind me of the fact. I want to pay because you've done so much for me and Mum over the last few days. This is simply a little 'Thank You'. There's no need to make a

153

big deal of it.'

She wasn't really trying to remind him; it was herself she was having to remind.

'Okay. I'm sorry. But there's no cause to get all stroppy. And I'm the one who should be saying 'Thank You'. If you and Vicky hadn't let me stay at her house, I don't know what I would've done. So where gratitude is concerned, I think I've got you beat.'

'I wasn't getting stroppy. And gratitude isn't necessary. That's what friends are for.'

'Right back at ya. *Friend*.'

'Why can't you just let me do something nice for you?'

'You've done lots of nice things for me over the last few days. Why can't you let me go halves?'

'Because I want ... to treat you.'

'That's lovely, Chance. But maybe I want to treat you. Have you thought about that?'

He raised his brows. 'Frankly, no.'

'Okay. This is getting silly. If it means so much to you, fine. You can pay. But only if you let me pay for drinks in here on New Year's Eve. Deal?'

'Deal.' He beamed at her, but a second later, the delight slipped from his face and an expression of abject horror replaced it. 'I can't, Molly. I ... I ... I'll be with Jolene on New Year's Eve.'

Molly's happiness melted away faster than

a snowman in sunshine. She had completely forgotten about Jolene. Yet again.

But so had he.

'Of course. Er. How silly of us. You'll be in your cottage on New Year's Eve, down on one knee, proposing to the woman you love. How could either of us forget about that? And we haven't even had any wine yet.'

Her laughter sounded hysterical but if she didn't laugh, she'd cry right now and she couldn't possibly do that. Even if her heart felt like a thousand angels were weeping inside it.

Chance looked as if he were trying to fathom out how he could've forgotten his soon-to-be fiancée so easily. He gave a small laugh, not quite as maniacal as hers, but close.

'I think we both got a little caught up in the moment.'

She nodded her head like a rapidly bouncing ball.

'And the argument. We both wanted to win. Or at least to come out equal.'

'Yes. Er. Shall we order?' He picked up his menu and hid his face behind it. 'Are you still having that turkey pie thing?'

'Turkey pie thing?' She laughed again, but this time it sounded normal. 'It's not a *thing*. It's heaven on a plate.'

He lowered his menu a fraction and glanced over the top, his eyes crinkling at the corners.

'Really? A pie?'

'Yes, mister. A pie. You're such a heathen sometimes. Don't knock it till you've tried it. But you're not trying any of mine. So get your own.'

She held her menu right in front of her face and stuck out her tongue.

'I know you're sticking out your tongue at me. You used to do that with books when we were young.'

She lowered the menu and put it on the table, shaking her head in genuine astonishment.

'How do you remember so much from those days? It really amazes me.'

He shrugged. 'I suppose it was because being at your house was such an important part of my life. It's as if I've cherished every memory and put it in a special box in my head and my heart. Not locked away. Wide open, so that I can pull things out in a second. Does that make sense?'

Molly nodded. 'I think that's wonderful.'

'Things were pretty miserable at home, as you know. Mum and Dad were either arguing, or giving one another the silent treatment. I was always caught in the middle and felt as if they were trying to force me to take sides. Which of course Dad did, eventually. When Mum's drinking got worse, Dad started spending longer out of the house. For me, coming to your place was like breaking free of some prison or something. And your parents were a breath of fresh air. They always made me feel so welcome. And loved. I really felt loved in your house.'

'You were, Chance. We all loved you. Like a brother, in mine and Terry's case, of course.'

She'd loved him, but it hadn't been like a brother.

He didn't need to know that though. There were so many things he didn't need to know. But in a strange way, she almost wished he did.

He smiled. 'I promised myself that if I ever got married, I would never behave like Mum and Dad. I want a marriage like your parents had. I think I only saw them argue a couple of times and each one lasted for about five minutes. Either your mum or your dad would stop, look at the other person, and say, 'Truce'. And they'd kiss and make up. Terry and you would pull faces and laugh but to me, that was really something. That two people could put aside their differences and compromise because they loved one another so much.'

Molly swallowed the tiny lump in her throat. She still missed her parents and hearing Chance talk about them with such love and admiration brought tears to her eyes.

'They were deeply in love from the day they met until ... Well, I think they're still deeply in love, wherever they are.'

157

'Oh, Molly. I didn't mean to upset you. I'm so sorry.'

She swiped away a solitary tear from her cheek and smiled.

'It's fine. It's wonderful to know they meant so much to you too. But if we could change the subject that'd be good. I might end up a blubbering wreck otherwise. And me with mascara trickling down my face is not a pretty sight, believe me.'

'I think I'd disagree with that. You always look pretty.' He cleared his throat and turned his attention to the menu once again. 'But no. You're right. Er. I'm having 'The Three Wise Men'.

'Oooooh good choice. The trio of smaller pies. You won't regret it. The pies here are the best in Easterhill.'

'The menu is more extensive than I thought. Some of the choices here would give the poshest New York restaurant a run for its money. But the trio of pies does sound delicious. And comfort food is what's called for when it's snowing outside. Turkey, Port and Cranberry. Steak, Red Wine and Mushroom. And finally, Ham, Spiced Cider and Onion. Yum.'

Molly laughed. 'Does champagne go with all that? What am I saying? Champagne goes with anything.'

The food was delicious, as Molly knew it

would be, and Chance promised he'd never look down his nose at a pie again.

'You're right,' he said after just a few mouthfuls. 'These pies are heaven on a plate.'

'I'm always right. Especially when it concerns food. And Christmas decorations.'

'Yeah, yeah. I'll admit you were right.' He held up his glass of champagne. 'Here's to you and to always being right.'

Molly held up her glass. 'And here's to you and to being able to admit it.'

'Happy Christmas, Molly. I hope you get everything you've wished for.'

She knew she wouldn't. Chance was in love with someone else.

'Happy Christmas, Chance. I hope the same for you.'

She didn't. Not totally. She hoped it would continue snowing so that his girlfriend's flight would be cancelled and she wouldn't make it here in time for New Year's Eve.

But that was mean. He deserved to be happy. Even if that meant him being happy with someone else.

'I really do,' she added, knocking back her glass of bubbly as if she hadn't had a drink for a week.

Twenty-Two

It was still snowing as Chance and Molly walked home but the temperature had dropped and in parts, where the snow had been trodden down, the pavements were icy. Molly had almost slipped as they left the pub but Chance had caught her arm and he linked it through his without thinking. He wanted to keep her safe.

That wasn't all he wanted.

He had just had one of the best nights of his life. Possibly *the best* night. And yet he couldn't end the night the way he wanted – because he had a girlfriend.

All he could think about, as he and Molly made their way home, was how much he wanted to kiss her.

He'd thought about it on and off all evening. All afternoon too, if he were honest.

Especially when they'd put up the decorations in the cottage earlier and he, his mum and Molly, together with Miracle and Beauty, had danced around the room to

'Rocking Robin'. Molly had caught her foot in a string of fairy lights and tripped, grabbing him as she fell. He'd managed to save her and had pulled her into his arms.

For a moment it was as if the rest of the world had vanished and it was just her and him, their lips inches apart, their bodies pressed together. But Miracle and Beauty had leapt up at them, thinking it was a game. Vicky had roared with laughter. And so had Molly.

But for just a split second, he had thought he'd seen something in Molly's eyes that had made him think she wanted him as much as he wanted her.

And tonight, more than once, she'd looked at him as if he were her hero. The love of her life. The one man in the world she really wanted to be with. His heart had raced, his head had pounded; at one point he'd felt as if he couldn't breathe. He had to fight the urge to take her hand in his and pull her to him and kiss her.

Now, as they were walking home, surrounded by softly falling snow and twinkling fairy lights, her arm linked through his, her body brushing against his with every step, he wanted that even more.

He saw the mistletoe hanging in the porch and this time he didn't make an excuse to avoid it. Perhaps he'd had too much champagne and wasn't thinking straight, but why not? It was

Christmas Eve, after all.

He could kiss her. He could get his wish. Well, part of it at least. She wouldn't think anything of a kiss under the mistletoe. And it wouldn't be cheating, exactly. Even though, in his heart of hearts, that was why, until now, he had walked away. Kissing Molly would feel like cheating.

But he wouldn't mind if Jolene kissed someone under the mistletoe on Christmas Eve. Not in the least. It was tradition. It didn't mean anything.

And would one kiss really do any harm? Just one, brief kiss?

The front door opened and his mum beamed at them.

'Hello, you two. Have you had a lovely time?'

Molly seemed as surprised to see Vicky as Chance was. It was as if she too had been deep in thought and Vicky had startled her.

'Yes thanks,' he said, as casually as he could. 'The pies are delicious. Molly was right about that.'

'It was lovely,' Molly said, sounding almost sad.

'Well.' Vicky glanced up and pointed at the mistletoe. 'I think you two have been avoiding it but you're not going to get away with that tonight. It's Christmas Eve. I'm going to stand here until you say you'll do it.'

'Mum!' Chance tried to sound cross but inside he was thanking his mum for her insistence. Now he had to kiss Molly. 'Maybe Molly doesn't want me to kiss her.'

'I do! I mean. I don't mind. As Vicky says, it's Christmas Eve. And it's a tradition.'

Had she just said she wanted him to kiss her? His heart felt three times its normal size.

'Go on then, darling. We haven't got all night.' Vicky tutted.

'Okay, okay. Er. Are you going to stand and watch?'

Vicky grinned. 'Only for a second, to make sure you kiss. And I don't mean one of those half-hearted pecks, either. It's got to be a proper kiss or it doesn't count.'

He took a deep breath and licked his lips. They were suddenly feeling dry.

He was nervous.

Oh God. Please don't let me mess this up.

Please let this be a good kiss.

My best kiss ever.

I need to do this right.

I'll never get another chance.

Wait. What?

Molly had grabbed his coat collar and was pulling him towards her.

Without another thought, he swept her into his arms and kissed her.

And kissed her deeper.

With increasing passion.

His tongue was in her mouth.

His hands were inside her coat.

He wanted her so badly it hurt.

And then something in his head made him stop and pull away from her.

She looked as stunned as he felt.

'Molly, I ... I didn't mean to kiss you like that.'

He glanced around in horror but his mum wasn't there. The front door was closed. Had she seen all that? Had she witnessed her son cheating on his girlfriend?

'It's okay, Chance.' Molly's voice sounded small. Croaky. Lost. 'I think we've both had too much champagne. Let's not mention this again. Please.'

He nodded even though her head was bowed and she wouldn't see it.

'I agree. You're shivering. Let's get inside.'

He opened the door for her and followed her in, watching her take off her coat, almost as if she were in a trance.

'Good night. Thanks for this evening. Say good night to Vicky for me.'

'Aren't ... aren't you coming through to the sitting room?' He was genuinely surprised. 'We were going to open a present each. To spend time with Mum. She'll be disappointed.' He'd be disappointed too.

'Oh.' Molly looked torn. 'I forgot.' She stood upright, pushed back her shoulders, avoiding his eyes. 'Yes, of course. But only for a little while, if that's okay. I … I'm getting a bit of a headache.'

'I'll get you some tablets and some water.'

'Thanks.'

He watched her go to join Vicky, and dashed to the kitchen. He splashed his face with cold water and gulped a glassful down. He opened the cupboard to find the tablets, filled a fresh glass with water, and after taking a couple of deep breaths, marched into the sitting room to join the two women he loved the most in the world.

His mum. And Molly Ford.

Only perhaps not in that order.

And definitely not in the same way.

He had never loved anyone, he was beginning to realise, in the way he loved Molly.

And that, quite clearly, was one heck of a monumental problem.

In exactly one week from today, he was supposed to be proposing to someone else.

Twenty-Three

Molly had no idea what she should do as she walked into the sitting room to join Chance's mum. She couldn't just pretend that nothing had happened tonight. To act as if she and Chance were just good friends. Not now. Especially not after that kiss.

Why did Chance have to be so bloody gorgeous?

And so damn nice.

And such an incredible kisser.

That kiss had nearly blown her mind. She'd felt things she'd never felt before and in places she never knew about. It was as if that kiss had transported her to another world. Some magical place where only she and Chance existed.

She'd even forgotten about Vicky. Although, thankfully, Vicky had left them to it.

But what must his mum think? Chance had a girlfriend. Almost a fiancée and here was some stupid girl who once lived around the corner, kissing her son as if her life depended on it. As if she would never let him go.

And if Chance hadn't suddenly pulled away, the plain fact was, Molly would've happily made love with him right there on the bloody doorstep. Even if Vicky had stayed.

Bloody hell. What on earth was wrong with her?

But why had Chance pulled away?

Was it just because he had a girlfriend?

Or was it because he could feel just how much Molly wanted him? And he didn't reciprocate her longing. Or her passion. Or her love.

Because that was the long and short of it. When you got right down to it. She was in love. In love with Chance bloody Warren. A man who in exactly one week's time would be down on one knee proposing to some other bloody woman.

And she wasn't just in love. And this wasn't just some holiday romance. This wasn't just because it was Christmas and she'd let herself get caught up in all the magic of the season.

No. This was real. This was true. And she wasn't just in love. She was madly, deeply, passionately in love.

For all the bloody good that would do her.

'Did you have a good time?' Vicky asked.

You. Have. Got. To. Be. Kidding. Me.

How could Vicky ask that as if she were

asking someone if they were enjoying a nice cup of hot chocolate? Didn't she see that kiss?

'Yes thanks,' Molly somehow managed. 'But I think I might've had too much champagne. I'm getting a bit of a headache.'

'Oh no, sweetheart.'

Vicky was genuinely concerned and Molly felt bad about lying. She didn't have a headache. But she did think her mind might implode. Or explode. Or whatever.

'Chance is getting me some tablets. But if you don't mind, I'll only stay for a few minutes and then I'll go to bed.'

'Of course I don't mind. We'll open one present each right away and then you can go and get some sleep. You'll want to be all bright-eyed and bushy-tailed for tomorrow. You're having breakfast here, aren't you, before going to your brother's for the day?'

If she didn't die of a broken heart in the night, yes.

'Er. Yes. That was the plan.'

'Excellent. At least Chance and I will get to spend some time with you on Christmas Day. And don't you worry about Miracle. He'll be fine here all day. Oh, and in case I forget tomorrow, when you want to leave Terry's tomorrow night, text Chance and he'll come and walk you home. Won't you darling?'

'Won't I what?'

Chance went straight to Molly and handed

her the tablets and the water but he avoided meeting her eyes.

'You'll go and meet Molly at her brother's tomorrow night so that you can walk her home.'

'Er ... Yes. Yes, of course I will.'

'There's really no need. It's just around the corner. I'll be fine.'

'It may be just around the corner,' Vicky said. 'But I'm not having you walking the streets on your own, late at night, especially with all the drunks you get at this time of year. And I'm speaking as a former drunk myself, don't forget. Most people mean well and are out to have fun, but sometimes, just sometimes, people go a bit too far. And it's a prime time for muggers and thieves, you know. I heard it on one of the documentaries. Or did I read it online? I can't recall. But anyway. Chance will come and meet you and that's the last we'll say about that. Now let's open a present each so that you can go and rest your pretty head. And I know I said this earlier, sweetheart, but you do look beautiful tonight. Especially in that gorgeous, and rather sexy dress.'

'Mum. You're forgetting Molly has a headache. I think you've said enough.'

'Oh, Pah. Go and get the presents from the tree and we'll let her get to bed.'

Vicky reached across and squeezed Molly's

hand, making Miracle and Beauty, who were both curled up with her on the loveseat, as usual, slip from their positions of comfort, bark, jump down and tear around the room.

Unfortunately for Chance, he didn't see them coming, and both Miracle and Beauty thumped into him, taking his legs from under him. Luckily, he fell back on an armchair, but he did a sort of sideways tumble, rolled off the chair and landed on his knees at Molly's feet.

She couldn't help herself and burst out laughing, as did Vicky. Even Chance laughed, once he'd obviously seen the funny side, but he glanced up at Molly, met her eyes and leapt upright as though the floor were on fire.

'Thank goodness that happened before you picked up the presents,' Vicky said. 'You might've broken something.'

'Thanks for the concern, Mum. I'm fine, in case you were wondering.'

'Of course you are, darling. I can see that. Now stop fooling around and get those presents. You're forgetting Molly's got a headache and wants to go to bed. Beauty. Miracle. Come here.'

To Molly's astonishment, both dogs stopped, looked at Vicky and trotted over to her like innocent little lambs. Which for an Olde English Sheepdog the size of a giant rug and a long-legged stray like Miracle, was no mean feat.

Chance chose one present for each of them from beneath the tree.

'Don't forget Beauty and Miracle,' Molly said, half-expecting him to say no one had bought presents for the dogs, even though she had.

'I won't. I just thought it might be safer for us to open our presents first.'

He handed one to his mum and one to Molly. She couldn't help but notice he'd chosen a present from him to her when she turned over the beautiful, sparkly pink tag and saw, 'To Molly. Merry Christmas. From Chance. Xx'

She couldn't hide her blushes but was glad he'd added kisses. She'd added kisses to her presents to him. But she'd also added the word Love, as in 'Love from Molly'. That made her feel a bit embarrassed. But she put that on all her presents.

'In case that's a present from me, I always put 'Love from Molly' on my gifts.'

Now that was really dumb. Both Chance and Vicky were looking at her as if they weren't certain why she'd said that.

'I do the same on mine, sweetheart. Except mine say they're from me, of course, not from you.'

Vicky laughed at her own joke and carefully peeled away the beautiful wrapping of the large, squidgy-looking present she was holding, which from the way it was wrapped in

171

a similar fashion to Molly's, was no doubt from Chance.

'Is it a new dressing gown? Or a super-soft towel?'

'Why don't you wait until you open it and see.'

Chance smiled at her as she continued the unwrapping.

'Oh darling. It's beautiful. I love it. Thank you so much.'

She held up a photo blanket, large enough to cover her and the loveseat, and it was a picture of her and Beauty snuggled up together, right where she sat.

'That's wonderful. And such a perfect present,' Molly said, meaning every word.

'Isn't it?' Vicky had tears in her eyes. 'Chance is always putting one of the throws over me when I nod off here, but none of them is large enough. This is perfect. Absolutely perfect. You're the best son ever, darling.'

'I'm really glad you like it.'

Vicky wrapped her new photo blanket over her and she and Chance looked at Molly.

'Oh. Am I next?'

She gingerly unwrapped her present, her heart thumping and her fingers not quite working as well as they should. Chance had bought her this, and whatever it was, she would treasure it. It was long and slim. A bracelet in a box, perhaps?

'I put a lot of thought, time and effort into that so I really hope you like it,' he said.

Her mouth fell open and her heart withered just a tiny fraction, but she knew it was a joke. And he had told her he'd get her a bar of chocolate, so she shouldn't be surprised that he had. Two bars, in fact.

'Yum. Just what I hoped for. And two bars? You shouldn't have. I don't deserve it.'

Vicky laughed too as Chance handed Molly another present. A rounder, heavier present that definitely wasn't chocolate.

Or was it?

'You get to open two because that was just a joke present,' he said.

She glanced at Vicky who nodded and back at Chance who was smiling at her.

This time she tore at the paper. She couldn't bear the suspense. And when she saw what it was, she couldn't speak at all.

He had bought her a snow globe. But not just any snow globe. It was a snow globe just like one that she had accidentally broken when she was twelve. One side had a snowy mountain scene with snow-covered trees and one tiny rabbit sitting on his haunches, looking up at the moon. The other side was for a photo and when she turned it round, she couldn't stop the tears from welling up in her eyes.

He'd put a photo in it. And again, not just any photo. It was a photo of the last Christmas he had spent with them all those years ago. The last Christmas before her mum and dad had died, eight months later, in a plane crash in the twin-propped light aircraft that they had clubbed together to buy as a joint present for each other that year because they both loved flying.

The photo was taken in the snow-covered garden of their former, family home, and it was of her mum, dad, Terry and herself. And Chance stood between her and Terry, and she noticed now, he was holding her hand. And her Golden Retriever, Belter was there too, sitting in front of her wearing a Santa hat on his head and a sparkly pink bow tie on his collar. Her beloved dog had also died the following year.

'I hope the photo hasn't upset you, Molly,' Chance was saying, his voice anxious and tender.

She looked into his eyes despite her tears.

'Absolutely not! Oh, Chance. It's made me so happy I think I might have to cry with joy. I loved this photo. Most of ours got lost when the house was sold and we moved in with our aunt and uncle. I didn't know you had a copy. This is the best present I've ever had. Honestly. I truly mean that. I can't believe you've done this for me.'

She jumped up and hugged and kissed him without even thinking. It wasn't a proper kiss, but she did kiss him on the mouth and when she realised what she'd done, she sat back down and cuddled the snow globe to her heart, smiling sheepishly at Vicky.

Now the present she'd bought for him, which he was about to open, paled in comparison.

But the massive smile on his face and the pure joy in his eyes comforted her.

'I don't believe it, Molly! It's as if we both had the same memory. I love this. Thank you doesn't cover it. And when it's built it's taking pride of place in my new home.'

She had bought him a model kit of the *Millennium Falcon*, the famous star ship from his beloved *Star Wars*. It was just like the model her mum and dad had bought for him that same last Christmas and that her dad and Terry had helped him build. The model that Belter, her dog, had broken a piece off, and her dad had stuck back on. Chance had pretended it hadn't mattered that his cherished model was no longer pristine, but she had known he was upset about it, even though at the time, she couldn't understand why.

Now Chance was coming towards her as if he was going to kiss her and she wasn't sure what to do. She had kissed him in thanks so it was only fair that he would do the same. It was a little awkward though and she quickly stood up and coughed.

'I hope you won't mind if I go to bed now,'

she said, looking at Vicky instead of Chance. 'Thank you so much for this evening, and my present and everything, but my head is getting worse. I'm sorry to spoil things.'

'You're not spoiling anything,' Vicky and Chance said in unison.

'Go to bed,' Chance said, with genuine tenderness in his voice. 'I hope you feel better and we'll see you in the morning.'

'Sleep well.' Vicky blew her a kiss.

'Thank you. Good night. And Merry Christmas.'

She hurried to the door, suddenly remembering the dogs were supposed to be opening presents and wondered if she should stay and do that, but neither Vicky nor Chance had mentioned it and she needed to get to her room. Her emotions were all over the place and she didn't think she could hold them in much longer.

'Molly.'

Chance was behind her as she reached the bottom stair and even though his voice was gentle, he startled her.

'Yes?'

She turned to look at him and wished she hadn't.

He covered the distance between them in two long strides and took her in his arms.

This time his kiss was soft and tender, not deep, desperate and passionate as it had been on the doorstep, but it still made her head spin and her heart race and her mind blank out all thoughts of anything other than him.

But once again, he pulled away, just as it was starting to get more intense.

He ran a hand through his hair.

'I only wanted to say thanks again and to wish you pleasant dreams.' He shook his head. 'I'm not sure how that happened.'

'It's Christmas, Chance. We've both been drinking and after those presents, we're both, understandably, feeling very emotional.'

'I knew I should've stopped at the two bars of chocolate.'

He laughed but it sounded forced.

'I'm glad you didn't. This present means the world to me. I was telling the truth when I said it's the best present I've ever had.'

'And yours means the world to me. I need to tell you something, Molly. But I don't know where to start. And it's not really the right time. But I think it should be said.'

'There's no need, Chance. I know. You told me, remember?'

She had to stop him before he said any more. She was certain he was attracted to her. Very much so, in fact. But she also knew he had a girlfriend. A girlfriend he loved and wanted to marry.'

'I did?' He looked confused. 'When? How?'

'Last Friday. The night you offered me and

Miracle a place to stay.'

'Last Friday? But … I only realised myself today, I think.'

'What? You told me last Friday that you were going to propose to your girlfriend on New Year's Eve.'

'Oh that. I'm not talking about that. Well, I suppose I am. In a roundabout way.'

'Look Chance. I like you. I really do. And you like me. We both know that. But we also both know you're as good as engaged.'

'We do?'

'Yes. And nothing can happen between us.'

'It can't?'

'No. Please don't worry or feel bad about tonight and that kiss. Both kisses. As I said, it's been emotional. And it's the season for love and romance so it's sort of understandable that, because we've been spending a lot of time together, we'd think things might be different when really they're not.'

'What? Run that by me again please.'

She shook her head. 'No. I think the less we say about tonight and those kisses, the better. We both know they shouldn't have happened. We both got a bit carried away. But there's no harm done and Jolene will never hear about them from me. I promise you that. Besides, a couple of kisses are no big deal, are they?'

'They aren't?'

'No. Lots of people kiss like that at this

time of year and it doesn't mean a thing.'

'It doesn't?'

'Absolutely not. I mean it's not as if we had full-on sex or anything.'

She coughed as an image of that popped into her head. Chance just looked utterly confused.

'No. We definitely haven't done that.'

'And we never will. I think we should both get a good night's sleep and forget those kisses. This time next week, you'll be engaged and I'll be packing to head home to Bristol. Good night, Chance. And thank you again for my wonderful present.'

She turned on her heel and ran upstairs before he had a chance to say anything further.

Twenty-Four

More snow fell during the night and Chance woke up on Christmas morning to find everything blanketed in a deep layer of white.

He stared out of his window and wondered how things had got so crazy. This time last week, he was doing up a cottage and planning a comfortable future with Jolene. The only worry on his mind was whether his mum's upcoming operation would be a success. He wouldn't have said he was excited about the path his life was taking, but he would've said he was reasonably happy with it.

Now, after spending the week with Molly and her mad dog, Miracle, his life had been turned upside down.

When he thought about his future, it wasn't Jolene he saw, it was Molly. And the thought of a future with Molly did excite him. Greatly. A lot more than he'd ever imagined possible.

When he thought about Molly, and he did

that far more than he'd realised until last night, his heart beat faster, his pulse throbbed, his head spun, and the blood in his veins felt as if it were on fire. And when he saw her, or heard her laugh, she both quenched that fire and yet stoked it to greater intensity.

He burned for her, he yearned for her, he gasped for her. He heard her voice, her laugh, her footsteps everywhere. He felt her touch, her breath, her kiss. Oh God, that kiss. Both kisses. He'd never kissed or been kissed like that. Ever. And somehow he knew that he never would be again. Unless he could be with Molly.

And he thought she felt the same. Or at least he hoped she did. Even if she felt for him half of what he felt for her, he'd be over the moon. But she'd stood on the stairs last night and stopped him from telling her how he felt about her.

She'd told him it was just because it was Christmas. Just because they'd had too much champagne. Just because they were feeling emotional.

Damn right he was feeling emotional. He'd never felt this emotional in his life. He'd learnt at a very young age not to show his true emotions. He didn't want his mum to be upset if he favoured his dad, or his dad to feel hurt if he favoured his mum, so he'd found a way to level out his feelings. To suppress them to a certain degree. To be easy going and level

181

headed.

With Jolene he could roll along comfortably and sedately.

With Molly his emotions shot to the moon repeatedly. There was nothing comfortable or sedate about being with Molly.

No. That wasn't entirely true. He did feel comfortable with her. But it was a completely different type of comfort. When he was with Molly he felt as if he were home. A field in Outer Mongolia would feel like home if Molly were there with him.

This must be what his mum had meant when she'd said that Love should be so much more than comfortable. Finally, he understood.

But it didn't really matter how he felt because last night Molly had made it perfectly clear. She didn't feel that way about him and this time next week, she'd be packing to leave to go home to Bristol and she assumed he'd be engaged to another woman and that hadn't seemed to bother her one bit.

He showered and dressed and went downstairs to make coffee. He needed it. He hadn't slept at all last night.

'Happy Christmas, darling!'

'Happy Christmas, Mum. You're up early. And Molly! You're up too. Er. Happy Christmas.'

'Happy Christmas, Chance.'

She was smiling but somehow she didn't look happy. Perhaps she still had her headache from last night.

'How're you feeling this morning, Molly?'

'Fine thanks. You?'

'Good, thanks.'

'Have you seen the weather?' She gave him another wan smile.

'Yeah. I can't believe how deep the snow is.'

'Neither can I.'

Okay. This was ridiculous. This was the type of conversation he and Jolene would have, not him and Molly.

'Are you two hungover?' Vicky asked. 'It's Christmas! We should be singing carols and ripping open presents.'

'You feel free to do that, Mum. I didn't get much sleep last night. Singing might be a big ask.'

Molly nodded. 'Same here.'

'Let's have breakfast. You'll both feel better with some smoked salmon blinis inside you.'

'Smoked salmon blinis for breakfast?' Chance wasn't sure he fancied that. 'I think I'll just have toast.'

'Me too,' Molly said. 'Shall I make it?'

'No. I'll do it. You're our guest.'

'For pity's sake, you two. Why don't you both go back to bed and get up again and start over?'

Chance yawned. 'I might do that.'

He could do with some sleep. Looking at Molly was making his stomach do crazy things. Not to mention his heart.

She was wearing a plain red skirt and a matching Christmassy jumper and her hair was hanging loose around her face and shoulders. She was leaning an elbow on the kitchen table and had one hand in her hair and the other was clenching a mug.

She looked so damn sexy that he wanted to sweep her into his arms and carry her up to his bed.

He might, if he had the energy to do so.

Which he doubted.

And she wouldn't want him to, so he couldn't.

'You can't go back to bed,' Vicky said. 'Not yet anyway. Molly's going to Terry's in half an hour and we've got more presents to open.'

'In half an hour? Fine. I'll make the toast and we'll do that.'

'Actually, I'm not really hungry. I think I'll skip breakfast.'

'Well, this is enough to send me back to the bottle!' Vicky exclaimed. 'Oh! Don't the pair of you look at me like that. I'm joking. I'm not giving up on all these years of sobriety just because the two people I love most in the world have both got their grumpy knickers on.'

Had his mum just said she loved Molly? From the look on Molly's face, she'd heard that too.

'Sorry, Mum.'

'Sorry, Vicky.'

'I should think so too. I could be dead in a month you know. And don't even think of giving me a lecture about not making jokes about such things, Chance. Because I don't want to hear it. Now slap a smile on your face, the pair of you, and let's go and unwrap some presents.'

Beauty and Miracle were both fast asleep on Vicky's loveseat but their heads shot up and their tails wagged as soon as Vicky walked in.

Chance loved the fact that Miracle had settled in so well and whatever happened in the future, he was sure about one thing – Miracle would always have a home with either his mum, or if, God forbid the worst happened, with him.

'Move over my darlings and let Mummy sit down.'

Vicky wiggled her bottom in front of the dogs and they both shifted over to make room for her.

Molly burst out laughing before giving Vicky a genuinely, loving smile.

'They both adore you. And I can see why.'

'Thank you, sweetheart. And I adore them both. I don't know what you've decided to do about Miracle, but if you can't take him with you, I'm happy to give him a home. For however long I may be here.'

Chance tutted but he laughed and rolled his eyes.

'And if Mum kicks the bucket – which she won't until I'm old and grey, both Beauty and Miracle will come to live with me. Unless you say otherwise, Molly. And you can visit whenever you like.'

'Thank you both,' Molly said. 'That's such a weight off my mind. I'd love to take him with me but the plain truth is I have to go out to work. He seems to have settled here and perhaps he'd be as calm as this if he came with me, but I somehow doubt it. And for his sake, I'd rather not take that risk. Knowing he'd be happy here, and loved and spoilt rotten, means such a lot.'

'That's settled then,' Vicky said. 'We'll contact the powers that be, once the holidays are over, and we'll get the adoption process rolling. Now hand out those presents, darling before we're all old and grey.'

Chance was surprised and delighted to discover that, in addition to last night's present, Molly had also bought him a pair of socks, one saying 'Left' and one saying 'The Other Left', plus a book on interior design.

'As a joke,' she said.

She'd got him a mug with 'World's Best Builder' emblazoned on both sides, as well, which also glowed in the dark.

He loved it when she roared with laughter as she opened his other joke present to her which was a white, winceyette vest and a matching pair of full, high waisted, winceyette knickers.

'I couldn't help myself,' he said. 'I had to buy you some 'sexy' underwear.'

And in his eyes, Molly would even look sexy in that.

He almost cried when his mum opened her present from Molly. It was a voucher for cream tea for two in Kew Gardens, one of Vicky's favourite places, and Molly had added a card and written on it, 'Not to be used until next summer'.

He knew it was Molly's way of saying that she wanted Vicky to have something lovely to look forward to, and to also tell Vicky that Molly expected her to still be around next summer. That positivity was so good for his mum.

Molly had also bought Vicky a silver photo frame and she'd put a photo of Vicky, Beauty and Miracle all asleep on Vicky's loveseat. Molly must've taken that the other day and had it printed for the size of the frame.

Vicky did cry and she beckoned Molly over to her and hugged her as if she truly loved her. Which did bring a tear to Chance's eye and he quickly dashed to the kitchen on the pretence of them all needing hot chocolate.

By the time he came back, Molly was nearly in tears. She was hugging the silver locket that he knew his mum had bought for her, but what he hadn't known was that Vicky had put a photo of him hugging Miracle, inside it.

'When did you take that?' he asked.

'When you didn't think anyone was looking,' Vicky said. 'I wanted Molly to remember that Miracle would be loved, no matter what.'

'But that must've been before you knew I might be looking after him.'

'I know a lot of things you might not think I know, darling.'

Molly's phone beeped and she checked the screen, letting out a small sigh and shoving it back in her bag.

'I'm afraid I've got to go. That's the third text Sarah has sent to ask how much longer I'll be. I think she wants to start opening presents and Terry's probably said they've got to wait for me. Thank you both for my truly wonderful gifts.'

'We haven't opened the dogs' presents yet,' Vicky said. 'But don't worry about that. Chance and I will give them one each and we'll wait until you get back tonight to give them the rest.'

'I'm not sure when that'll be. Five more minutes won't hurt. Let's open a couple now.'

Beauty and Miracle were thrilled with their

treats, their toys and their bones that Chance and his mum had bought, and they loved the new beds from Molly. Although Miracle didn't seem sure if he wanted to eat his, to pee on it, or sleep on it, but when he saw Beauty curl up and look very regal on hers, he promptly did the same on his. Although his droopy eyes gave the impression that he really wasn't bothered.

When she got up to leave, Molly hugged Miracle and kissed him on the head.

'I love you, you mangy, manic mutt. It was certainly a miracle when you came into my life.'

Chance couldn't help wishing she would say the same to him.

Only without the mangy, manic mutt, part.

Twenty-Five

Sarah and Terry opened the door together and shouted, 'Surprise!' as Sarah stuck her left hand in front of Molly's face.

Molly couldn't believe her eyes. The diamond solitaire was huge. Terry must've been saving for years to afford it.

'Congratulations!' Molly shrieked, jumping up and down in the snow.

'Come in, come in,' Sarah said, clearly unable to contain her excitement.

'When did this happen?' Molly asked. 'This morning?'

Sarah shook her head so vigorously that Molly thought it might fall off.

'Last night. At the restaurant. He'd had the ring put in a Christmas cracker and when we pulled it, he made sure I won and got the end with the prize in it. I honestly thought it was one of those Christmas cracker rings but couldn't believe how much it sparkled and I was just beginning to realise that it was a real diamond when he got down on one knee and proposed. Oh Molly, it was so romantic. The entire restaurant cheered and clapped and we drank champagne. Lots of champagne and we came back here and had the best sex we've ... oh. I wasn't supposed to tell you that bit.'

Sarah laughed and Terry rolled his eyes before pulling his fiancée into his arms and kissing her.

Molly hugged them both, overcome with happiness, completely forgetting she'd been freezing cold just a moment ago after her walk from Vicky's house in the snow.

'You're dripping melting snow all over the floor,' Terry said, laughing. 'Give me your coat and stuff and go into the sitting room. I'll get a bottle of champagne from the fridge and we can celebrate properly. Oh, and Merry Christmas!'

Molly beamed at Terry. 'Merry Christmas.'

She hugged him again before shrugging off her coat and handing him that, together with her tasselled red hat and matching scarf and gloves.

Sarah was laughing ecstatically. 'Merry Christmas! I'd almost forgotten about it.'

Molly linked arms with her and they hurried towards the roaring fire in the cosy sitting room as Sarah told her their plans for a summer wedding.

'That soon? I mean it's not that soon. But from a planning point of view it sort of is. Can you organise the wedding of your dreams in six months? And can you get the church and the reception venue in time?'

'No idea,' Sarah said. 'But if we can't, we'll find somewhere else. I honestly don't care where we get married, I just don't want to wait too long. I know we live together so it really shouldn't matter, but it does. I want to be Terry's wife, not just his partner or his girlfriend.'

'You're his fiancée now.'

'Oh yes. I am, aren't I? I can say things like, 'my fiancé and I did this', or 'my fiancé and I had sex in the bath.'

'I don't think you should say that.' Terry laughed, reappearing with the champagne. 'But I like the sound of 'my fiancée'. I can say things like, 'my fiancée loves me so much that she lets me watch football on Christmas Day.'

Sarah grinned. 'You could say that. But it wouldn't be true. At least not the football part.'

Molly gave him a playful slap on the arm. 'Bad luck, brother dear. But nice try.'

'I forgot the glasses.' Terry chuckled as he went back to the kitchen to get them.

'There's just one thing I have to know,' Sarah whispered. 'Did you tell Terry what I said? He says he knew nothing about that conversation and that he's been planning this for weeks. That's true, isn't it? Please say it is.'

'It's true. I didn't say a word and I know

Chance wouldn't have. And Terry did tell me months ago that he wanted to take you out somewhere special this Christmas Eve and that I'd have to spend the evening here on my own. I thought it was just to celebrate four years together. He didn't tell me he was going to propose. Which I'm a bit miffed about now I think of it.'

'What are you miffed about?' Terry asked, glasses in hand.

'Er.' Sarah was shaking her head and pulling faces so Molly had to think of something fast. 'That Chance is planning to propose to his girlfriend on New Year's Eve. Did you know about that?'

'What? No. Are you sure?'

'Absolutely. He told me himself. Oh. But he did say he hadn't told anyone apart from his mum. Damn I've done it again.'

'Done what again?'

'Nothing, Terry. Pour the bubbly. I could die of thirst here.'

'You're so bossy, sis. But why are you miffed about Chance proposing?'

Sarah tutted. 'Because she's falling in love with him herself, isn't that obvious?'

'Is it?' Molly queried.

'Molly's falling in love with Chance? Are you sure?'

They all exchanged glances and Terry handed round the glasses of champagne.

'As it happens, I'm not falling in love with him. It's too late for that. I've fallen. Hook, line and sinker. Head over heels. Madly, passionately, deeply.'

'Okay, we get the picture.' Terry rolled his eyes. 'When did this happen? I know you had a crush on him when we were young. And he had a crush on you. But Love? That's new.'

Molly shook her head. 'I think I've always been a little in love with him. But now I *know* I am. And totally.'

'It's true,' Sarah confirmed. 'She has. At least she has ever since I've known her. She just thought it was lust. She didn't realise it was love. Don't you remember how cross she always got when you told her Chance was coming over and she wasn't able to get here in time?'

'Yes but ... Oh, I see. Wow! Why didn't you tell me?'

Molly raised her brows and nodded towards Sarah's ring. 'Ditto.'

'That's different. I needed it to be a secret until last night.'

'I wouldn't have said anything. I'm a little offended by that.'

'Yes. I can see how wrong it was of me not to tell you. Remind me again. How many people have you told about Chance's secret upcoming proposal?'

'Ah. That's different.'

'I'm sure Chance wouldn't think so.'

Sarah nodded. 'And you have only known about that for a week. Imagine if Terry had told you months ago.'

Molly let out a sigh and pouted her lips. 'Okay, okay. So I'm not always good at keeping secrets. By the way, Terry, please don't tell Chance you know.'

Terry burst out laughing. 'What are we going to do with you, Molly?'

'Kill me. But in the meantime, let's toast the happy couple. Congratulations you two. Wishing you good health, great wealth and True Love and Happiness always.'

'I'll drink to that,' Terry said.

'Me too,' said Sarah. After taking a few sips she added, 'I think we need to find Molly a boyfriend. And fast.' She reached out and squeezed Molly's hand.

'Why? She loves Chance. She just told us so.'

'Try to keep up, Sherlock,' Molly said. 'Chance is about to propose. And it's not to me. It's to his current girlfriend.'

Terry sighed. 'For one thing, have you seen the weather out there? Or heard the forecast? Airports are closed. Flights are cancelled. Even if he wanted her to come over, I'm not sure she could get here. For another thing, if he was genuinely in love with ... whatshername, why is he spending every waking hour possible with you? Why did he invite you to his place to stay? And why did he take you out for dinner last night?'

'I told him about that last bit,' Sarah said.

'We won the Snowball Pie event, remember? We were simply using the vouchers.'

'On Christmas Eve. Come on.'

'I'm not saying he doesn't like me, Terry. I'm pretty sure he does. If those kisses were anything to go by, he likes me a lot.'

'Wait. What? Back up there a minute.' Sarah swung round on the sofa and tucked her knees under her, turning to face Molly and nearly spilling her drink in the process. 'What kisses? I haven't heard about any kisses.'

Molly sighed wistfully. 'Because they happened last night.'

'Last night? H-ell-o. Why didn't you text me?'

'Er.' Molly pointed to Sarah's ring. 'Once again. Ditto.'

'This is different. Terry and I wanted to tell you together. And not by phone.'

'And I was going to tell you today. And I have.'

'Actually, you haven't. All you've said so far is "those kisses". I need details, like when? Where? What were you wearing, if anything?'

'Sarah! He's got a girlfriend.' Molly stretched out and slapped Sarah's hand. 'I shouldn't even have kissed the man. But I'd definitely draw the line at that.'

'He kissed you more than once?' Terry checked.

'Yes. Once under the mistletoe. But it was a really passionate kiss. Tongues and everything. I almost melted on the spot.'

Terry grinned. 'He clearly wasn't thinking about whatshername at the time. What *is* her name?'

'Jolene.' Sarah and Molly laughed as they sang out the name. 'Like in the song.'

Terry furrowed his brows. 'Whatever. And the second time?'

'In the hall. I was standing on the bottom stair and he came to thank me for my presents and he kissed me instead. Oh. You won't believe what he gave me.' She rummaged in her bag. 'I've brought it with me. Look. Do you remember this, Terry? Of course you do. What am I saying?'

Terry studied the snow globe.

'I think you had ... oh my God!' He saw the photo. 'Sarah, look. This was taken on Christmas Day the year before Mum and Dad died. Where did he get it, Molly?'

'He had a copy all this time. Mum or Dad must've given it to him, I suppose because he's in it and they thought he might like it. And Sarah, the snow globe is just like one I had. But it got broken that year.'

Sarah beamed at her. 'He clearly did like the photo if he's kept it all these years. And you know what? If a man gave me a present like this I wouldn't be worried about his girlfriend. I'd be worried about his sanity. Because a man who's in love with someone doesn't give another woman a present like this. To find a snow globe like one he knew you had, and to put a treasured photo in it, well, do I really have to spell it out? The man's in love with you, Molly. He just may not realise it yet.'

'I wish that were true.'

'I agree with Sarah. My fiancée.' Terry blew Sarah a kiss. 'I would never give a present like that to a woman unless I was pretty crazy about her. And definitely not if I had a girlfriend.'

'But you're forgetting, Chance and I have been friends for years. That's different.'

'No, it's not,' Sarah said. 'If my boyfriend – now my fiancé – gave another woman that present, even if he'd been born on the same day as her and they had lived next door to one another all their lives, he wouldn't stay my fiancé. There are limits, Molly. And another thing. Chance told you himself that he's "not a photo kind of guy", didn't he? He hasn't even got a photo of his girlfriend and yet he's kept this photo all these years. And he must've had it with him, either in a frame somewhere, or on his phone and he's had it printed out. That's a pretty big deal.'

That was true. Chance had said that. And Sarah was right. It was a big deal.

'I don't know. But what can I do? I can't exactly ask him to dump his girlfriend, can I? What if he doesn't feel like that about me? What if he does just see me as a really close friend? We'd never be able to meet again. It'd be *sooooo* embarrassing.'

'But what if he does?' Sarah said.

'Wouldn't he say something?'

Terry nodded. 'If he thought there was a chance you felt that way about him. Yes. But as you just said yourself, what if he thinks you see him as merely a good friend? If he said he loved you and you said, 'Thanks, but I don't feel the same,' it'd be just as embarrassing for him.'

'I suppose it would. I didn't think of that. And last night, he did say that he needed to tell me something. I thought he was going to tell me about the proposal and that he'd forgotten he already had. But maybe he wasn't. Maybe he was going to tell me something else entirely.'

'There's only one way to find out,' Terry said. 'And by my reckoning, you've got five days in which to do that. Not counting today and New Year's Eve.'

'And you should do it sooner rather than later,' Sarah added. 'You need to give him time to dump Jolene before she gets on that plane. Assuming any are flying.'

Molly's tummy rumbled. 'We need to

devise a plan. But first I need to eat. What have you got for breakfast? And please don't say smoked salmon blinis.'

Twenty-Six

Christmas Day with Sarah and Terry was great fun, as it always was, but every so often throughout the day, Molly was missing Chance.

She kept wondering what he and Vicky were doing. Were they watching TV? Opening more presents? Reading? Taking the dogs for a walk in the deep blanket of snow?

Was he wondering what she was doing? Or was he video-calling Jolene and telling *her* how much he loved her and missed her and was counting the days until New Year's Eve?

Opening presents made her miss Chance, far more than she expected, but she loved the Christmas jumper Sarah had knitted her, and the reindeer embellished PJs from Terry. They'd also bought her a bottle of her favourite wine, a cook book she had wanted, and a gorgeous, glittery fountain pen she'd longed for months ago.

Christmas dinner took her mind off Chance for just a moment or two. It was delicious, mainly because Sarah was a brilliant cook.

Molly had helped peel the veg, and watched, as always, as Sarah worked her magic and when she was done, the table virtually groaned beneath the bounty laid on its Christmassy decorated top.

Carrots bathed in a mustard and sherry dressing with a sprinkle of toasted hazelnuts for good measure. Sausage, walnut and sage and onion stuffing made from a family recipe. The honey-glazed parsnips were cooked to perfection as were the pigs in blankets and a tray of baked sausage meat, which was one of Molly's favourites. Roasted sprouts with pistachios and chestnuts, and braised red cabbage with apples and cider, piled high in beautiful, Christmassy serving dishes, along with a large platter of rosemary and garlic, crispy roast potatoes, so golden that they almost glimmered.

Molly did make the Christmas trifle, adding far more sherry than she should, but hey. It was Christmas Day. There was day-old, homemade sponge cake, which Sarah had made on Christmas Eve and Molly had broken into pieces and drowned in sherry. On top of that, she added jelly and once that was set, she layered it with forest fruits and covered the whole lot in homemade custard before smothering it with cream, grated chocolate and multicoloured edible sprinkles. You had to have a bit of 'kitsch' at Christmas.

Sarah had also made a Christmas pudding, which she'd decorated with edible holly, using marzipan for the leaves and cranberries soaked in brandy for the berries. They removed the marzipan leaves before they lit the pudding, but they left the cranberries. The flames made them pop and sizzle as the mini fire encased the entire pudding in a cloak of blue, purple, gold and red before burning itself out having consumed all the brandy.

Sarah's Christmas cake was scrumptious, and her Yule Log was to die for. Molly joked that she'd eaten so much, she probably would.

Sarah had even gone so far as to make a special chocolate alternative, doggy Yule Log for Miracle. And one for Beauty too. She'd found the recipe on the internet on one of the animal welfare sites. That's how lovely Sarah was. Even though she was allergic, it didn't mean she didn't like dogs.

'They'll love these,' Molly said. 'Thanks Sarah. You're such a star. My brother is a very lucky man.' She glanced at Terry.

'There's no need to tell me, I know.'

Terry looked at Sarah with eyes filled with love.

Chance's eyes had looked a bit like that last night.

Did that mean …? Was it possible? No. She

must've imagined it. Chance wasn't in love with her. In lust, maybe. But he was in love with someone else.

But she couldn't stop wishing that he might fall in love with her. And preferably before New Year's Eve.

When she and Sarah pulled the turkey wish bone, on Terry's insistence, Molly wished that Chance would tell her he loved her. And when she got the winning half of the bone, she prayed that for once, this Christmas wish would come true.

After lunch they played Charades, Monopoly and Poker. Molly lost at all three.

'What's the saying?' Sarah asked. 'Lucky in Love, unlucky at cards.'

'And games,' Molly added. 'But I've never been lucky in Love, either. Does that make me a full-on loser?'

'You've been lucky in your career,' Terry said. 'Although a lot of that is down to talent and hard work.'

'Ah thanks, brother dear. That's the nicest thing you've ever said.'

'Don't be ridiculous. I say lots of nice things to you.'

That was true. He did. He'd always been a great support. He'd always been in her corner. And when their parents had died, Terry had been the one who had got her through their devastating loss.

Aunt Maggie and Uncle John had been wonderful. John was their dad's brother and was many, many years older than their dad. As was Maggie. About twenty years, in fact. Their dad had been 'a late surprise'. But they welcomed Terry and Molly into their home, even though they had chosen not to have children of their own, just dogs. Maggie and John had loved dogs.

Now they were both gone too. Why was it that so many good people died young? Not that Maggie and John were *that* young when they died. They had both been in their late seventies.

Since then, it had only really been Molly and Terry. Until Molly had met Ian, and thought she'd found 'The One'. She had moved to Bristol with Terry's blessing, only to realise Ian was far from being 'The One' after all.

But she'd built a life in Bristol and although she'd seriously considered moving back to Easterhill, for some reason, she had stayed.

The business had taken off and one weekend, she'd come to stay with Terry, gone to the Easterhill summer market, and met Sarah.

That had really made her think about moving back. But in a way, she thought it might interfere with the budding romance she could see unfolding between her brother and her friend. And she was happy in Bristol. She had friends. She dated on and off. Her business thrived. Plus, Easterhill was nowhere near the size of Bristol and having it to come back to for weekends now and then was actually rather nice.

But now, when she thought about going back to Bristol, she felt as if she'd be leaving her heart behind. And more than her heart. She felt as if she'd be leaving her true home.

Wishing Well Cottage would never be her home. She must stop wishing it might. But that didn't stop her picturing Chance playing catch in the snow-covered garden with Miracle. Or Chance lying in his bed looking up at the stars through those roof skylights.

Not that Chance had a bed yet. Molly knew that was one of the things that hadn't arrived. Vicky's offer for him to take his bed from her house still stood, but Molly was certain Chance wanted his new bed to turn up in time for New Year's Eve, when it would, obviously, be seeing a great deal of action. And that was something Molly really didn't want to think about.

The day flew by and before she knew it, it was almost ten.

'Chance is here,' Terry said.

'He is?'

She hadn't texted him. She had planned to walk home on her own, in spite of what Vicky had said.

Chance followed Terry into the sitting

room and Molly watched him as Sarah and Terry told him their wonderful news.

For a split second, when he'd seen the ring, he'd glanced in Molly's direction. Or perhaps she'd imagined he did.

'Congratulations!' He looked genuinely pleased. And why wouldn't he be?

'There's nothing quite like being in love,' Terry said, hugging Sarah tight. 'You should try it mate.'

'I ... Er ... Yes. I should.'

Again, had she imagined Chance had looked at her?

Terry opened more champagne and they toasted to True Love and Happiness and everything along the way.

Almost an hour later, after all four of them had yawned several times, Sarah suggested it was probably time they all went to bed.

And Chance had definitely looked at Molly that time. She was absolutely certain of it. Because he was still looking at her now. And he continued to look at her as she put on her coat and boots and as they left Terry's cottage and walked along the road. So much so that Molly couldn't help herself.

'Okay, Chance, what is it?' She stopped in her tracks in the snow. 'You've clearly got something on your mind. Are you going to spit it out?'

'Er.' He seemed startled and now he looked

away. 'You're right. I have.' He turned back and met her gaze. 'I know this is bad timing. And it's bloody inconvenient too. I realise that. But the thing is, Molly...' His phone rang and interrupted him and he cursed as he fumbled in his coat pocket to pull it out.

'Do you have to answer it?'

'It might be Mum.'

It obviously wasn't and by the expression on his face, Molly knew that it was Jolene. He hesitated for a second, his hand hovering over the screen.

'I'll walk on ahead. You catch up when you've finished.'

Without waiting, she marched off as best she could. She was both surprised and disappointed to find he wasn't walking behind her. When she glanced round to see where he was, he was leaning against a lamppost, his head drooping slightly, his phone looking as if it was stuck to his ear.

She reached Vicky's front door and there was still no sign of him behind her. Had something happened? Should she go back? Perhaps she should've waited.

She was about to turn back and go and look for him when he appeared at the end of the road. He was trudging through the snow as if he was having trouble walking. His head was bowed, his shoulders hunched and his hands were stuffed in his pockets. If ever a body had said, 'Don't come anywhere near me,' Chance's body did right now.

'Is everything all right?'

Her voice clearly surprised him. It was as if he hadn't expected her to be there. His eyes met hers, looked away, looked up to the mistletoe and down at the ground and when he spoke, the words were muffled by his coat and scarf.

'No. And it probably never will be again.' He gave a strange snort of laughter. As though it hurt him. 'Although I suppose I should be happy. I know Mum will be.'

'Chance? You're not making any sense. What's happened? Please tell me. I'm getting a little worried.'

He sucked in the deepest, longest breath she'd ever seen and his shoulders rose as did his head. He let out the breath in an even longer sigh.

'I've just been given the greatest gift ever, I suppose. And yet it doesn't feel like it.' He coughed loudly and ran a hand through his hair before he met her eyes. 'Jolene has ... has just informed me ... I'm going to be a dad.'

Twenty-Seven

Molly couldn't remember much about what had happened after Chance had broken his devastating news.

She could remember that she'd tried to run indoors but she couldn't get the door open. Chance had come to her aid and had whispered her name in a way that made her think his heart was breaking as much as hers was.

'Molly I...' he'd said. And then nothing. It was as if he'd been struck dumb.

Vicky must've heard the door rattling as Molly had tried to open it and she was in the hall as Molly had rushed past and fled upstairs. That was all she remembered, apart from phoning Sarah and crying her eyes out to Sarah and Terry.

Chance hadn't come to try to talk to her, and surprisingly, nor had Vicky, but Miracle had managed to open the door with his paws and had jumped onto her bed. For one brief moment she had hoped that it was Chance who was trying to open her bedroom door, but no such luck.

This morning, Vicky tapped on the door and came in before Molly had told her she could.

'Good morning, sweetheart. How are you today?'

Was she for real? She was behaving as though last night hadn't happened.

Perhaps it hadn't! Could that awful end simply have been a dream?

More like a nightmare!

Molly sat upright against the headboard and took the mug of coffee Vicky had brought her.

'Thanks for this.' She took a sip of the refreshing beverage. 'I'm not sure. How ... how are you?'

Vicky dropped onto the bed and sighed, taking Molly's free hand in hers.

'Surprised. Shocked. Thrilled and yet not. Happy and yet equally sad. Confused. Bewildered. Cross. I think that about sums it up.'

So it was true. It hadn't been a dream.

'For me too, I think.'

'And for Chance.'

'I ... I thought you'd be ecstatic. And so would he.'

'Perhaps if this had happened a week or two ago, I would've been. And so would he. But now...' She shrugged. 'I know I should be thrilled – and he knows he should be too, but I don't think I've ever seen him so torn up. Well, not since his father announced he was in love with someone else, and he and I broke up. Chance had to choose who to live with. That almost tore him apart.'

'I was always a little surprised by that.' Molly had no idea why she was saying this now. But then she wasn't really sure what she was saying, or feeling, or thinking. 'I thought he would've chosen you. Because you needed him the most and he was always there when anyone needed him. That's just the sort of boy he was.'

'And the sort of man he is. Nothing's changed, Molly. And I'll tell you something. He didn't choose his dad. He chose to stay with me. For precisely the reason you said. He knew I needed him more than his dad did. Which is why I couldn't let him do that. I made him go with his dad. I made his dad take him even though Chance was saying he wanted to stay. I might have been a drunk and at the time a very bad mother, but I couldn't do that to my beloved son. I couldn't ruin his life more than I had already. And I would've. Although Chance is strong and he would've adapted. But I don't think he would be quite the man he is today if he had had to deal with me on his own in those days.'

'I had no idea.'

'He's such a good man, Molly. And that's why this is breaking his heart. And mine. Because he'll marry Jolene, in spite of all the times he's said he never wants a marriage like the one his father and I had. He'll marry her because he feels he should. Because he won't want a child of his to be without a dad. He'll marry her even though he's madly in love with someone else who is, who was, and who always will be, the one True Love of his life.'

Molly met her eyes. 'Do you ... do you mean me?'

'Do you doubt it?'

'Yes! No. I don't know.'

'Yes you do, sweetheart. You know, deep down that he loves you. And you know that you love him.'

'I do know I love him. And I thought ... I hoped ... but I wasn't sure. I thought ... he might just love me as a friend. A really good friend.'

'He loves you so much more than he ever thought possible.'

'He's told you that?'

'He didn't need to. I could see it in the way he looks at you. The way he is with you. In everything he said and did. But yes. He told me that last night. Just after he told me about Jolene. We sat up for most of the night and talked. I tried to convince him that he could still be a good dad without marrying Jolene.

That he could be with you and be truly happy and still have his child in his life. But he said he didn't think he could do that. That it wouldn't be fair to anyone. He'd want to live near his child. He couldn't ask Jolene to come and live here if he wasn't going to be asking her to live with him. And he couldn't ask you to move to New York so that he could be near his child by another woman. He also said he didn't know if you even loved him but I soon put him right on that.'

'I ... I'd go to New York if he asked me. I'd go anywhere to be with him. I'd go to Mars if that's what he wanted.'

'I told him I thought you'd say that. But there is one thing about Chance that is really rather annoying. Bloody infuriating, actually. He can sometimes get an idea in his head that makes no sense at all to anyone other than him, and when he does that, it takes heaven and earth to make him change his mind. He can also, on occasion, be a bit of a martyr. For example, moving here to be near me. He has a wonderful life in New York and runs a hugely successful business but he finds out I am ill and what does he do? He immediately sells his business to a competitor who's wanted it for years, buys a run-down cottage, and moves, lock, stock and barrel back here just to spend time with me so that I won't be alone. Any 'normal' person would've hired a carer and come over to visit whenever he could, but not my Chance. Oh no. Nothing will do for him but to actually be here and hold my hand. I love him for it, don't get me wrong. But I don't want my son to put his life on hold for me. Or change it completely just to be nearby. Even though it's been a dream come true to have him here. And now he's going to try to do that for his child too. It makes no sense to me.'

'I ... I don't want to seem uncaring. Or say something out of place, but what will he do if ... if those two things collide?'

'If I'm still ill, or dying when his child is born, you mean?'

Molly nodded. She didn't want to say the words out loud.

Vicky shook her head. 'He'll try to do both and he'll no doubt wear himself out. Or end up having a heart attack from all the stress. To be honest, I have no idea and what's more, he doesn't either. That's something we'll have to deal with when it happens.'

'*If* it happens. I shouldn't have said anything. I'm certain your operation will be successful and you'll be up and about again in no time. Long before your ... your grandchild is born.'

'My grandchild.' Vicky sighed loudly. 'Sometimes life can be cruel, Molly. Just a few weeks ago if anyone had asked me, I'd have said I would give anything to see Chance happily

215

married and that to be a grandmother would be icing on my cake and a dream come true. But now all I can think about is that Chance should be with you and that this baby is more of a curse than a blessing. And that's a dreadful thing for me to say. But I know Chance will end up being miserable and yet nothing I've said so far will make him see that. Perhaps you can make him see sense.'

'I … I'm not sure I can do that. I don't want to try to make him do something he doesn't want to. I … I think, perhaps, if it's all right with you, I should go back to stay at my brother's. But that means I'd have to leave Miracle here with you and Chance.'

Vicky studied her face for a moment before smiling wanly. 'Miracle has a home with me for life, Molly. There is no need for you to worry about him. And you can come and stay whenever you like. And, wherever in the world Chance may be, whether that's here or in New York, if anything happens to me, Chance will give Miracle a home with him. That much I can promise you.'

'Thanks. I know that's true. And now I think I should get dressed and go.' She placed her mug on the bedside table and took Vicky's other hand in hers, squeezing both hands gently. 'Thank you so much for everything, Vicky. This was the best Christmas I've had for a long time. I'm just … well. There's no point in going into that. Will you … will you say goodbye to Chance for me, please? I really don't think I can face him today. Or any day soon come to that. My heart is breaking and if his is too, I know I couldn't bear it.'

'If that's really what you want, of course, sweetheart. But I think you two need to talk about this. I really think you do. But maybe not today. You're right. A few days apart might do you both some good. It might even make Chance see sense.'

Molly knew a few days apart wouldn't do her any good at all. But then neither would being here. With him. So close, and yet now even farther apart than ever.

After Vicky left her, she called Sarah and asked if she could go back to stay with them. Without Miracle.

'You can even bring him if that would help ease the pain,' Sarah said. 'I can live with a few sniffles and a runny nose. I've got plenty of tablets.'

'That's really kind, but we both know your allergy involves a lot more than sniffles and a runny nose, and I wouldn't inflict that on you again, no matter what.'

'How come you're being so calm? Isn't your heart breaking in two?'

Molly sighed heavily. 'Yes, Sarah. It is. But I think I'm still in a state of shock or something. None of this feels real. Not Chance telling Vicky he loves me. Not him being a dad. Not the fact that I'll never get the opportunity to tell him how I feel. None of it. It's like I'm watching some awful movie and I'm just waiting for it to end. It's almost as if I'm in a nightmare and I'm sure I'll wake up and things will be as they were last night. Before the call from Jolene. But can we talk about this later? I've got to get out of here. I can't risk bumping into Chance. I'm pretty sure that would tip me over the edge and I'd really lose it and collapse into a sobbing heap at his feet.'

Molly didn't bother to shower. She dressed and packed her bags and crept downstairs where Vicky was waiting in the sitting room, curled up on her loveseat with the dogs.

Molly hugged them all. Several times. It was breaking her heart to leave. She really didn't want to go. But she heard Chance moving about upstairs and that was it. She hugged them all again, said a last, 'Goodbye. I love you all', and fled as quickly and as quietly as she could, slipping and sliding in the deep snow in front of Vicky's house.

She was both astonished and grateful to see Sarah and Terry's car coming towards her and even more so when both Sarah and Terry jumped out.

'You've come to get me?'

'Of course we have.'

Sarah linked her arm through Molly's, and

Terry put Molly's cases in the back after giving his sister the biggest hug.

'I can't believe this is happening,' Terry said. 'But we weren't going to let you come home on your own.'

Before she could say a word, Molly burst out crying.

Emily Harvale

Twenty-Eight

Boxing Day dawned bright, and warm lemon
sunshine flooded Molly's bedroom in Terry's
cottage. The snow outside began to melt
rapidly as the temperature rose to an
unseasonal high.

By lunchtime, the roads were even
passable, if you had the right type of car for icy
conditions. The occasional snowdrift was still
clinging to one or two parts of the highway and
some of the pavements were treacherous in
places, according to the local news reports.

The day flew by without Molly realising
where it went, or really remembering much
about it.

She did remember that they had gone to
Seahorse Harbour to have a Boxing Day drink
with Asher Bryant, and to meet his new
girlfriend, Lottie Short in the only pub in the
village, The Seahorse Inn.

It was owned by a friend of Asher's, called
Mikkel Meloy, and Molly could remember

Sarah telling her in the car on the way, how gorgeous Mikkel was and that he had only recently become single again, after a break-up had left him with a broken heart.

'At least you'll have that in common,' Terry had said, somewhat unhelpfully.

'I've met Mikkel before,' Molly reminded them. 'He's gorgeous, I'll give you that, but if you think that throwing us together is a good idea, you're clearly both as mad as a pair of drunken reindeer. I can't believe you're even suggesting it.'

'We thought it might help you to know that you're not the only one going through this.' Terry gave her a comforting smile via the rear-view mirror.

Molly slumped further down on the back seat.

'Yeah. Nothing helps like knowing you're not alone in your misery. But crying with someone into my beer isn't exactly how I pictured spending my day. I wanted to stay in bed.'

'You don't drink beer,' Terry said.

'I think you're missing the point, darling.' Sarah tapped him gently on the arm.

He furrowed his brows and glared at Molly in the mirror.

'You stayed in bed all morning. You need fresh air and conversation.'

'I need chocolate ice cream, several boxes

of chocolates, and alcohol. At least I'll get the alcohol in Mikkel's pub. I hope he serves wine by the barrel.'

Sarah sighed. 'Perhaps this was a mistake.'

Truer words had never been said, as Molly pointed out to Sarah when they arrived a few minutes later at The Seahorse Inn to find not just Asher and his lovely girlfriend, Lottie, seated at a table in front of a roaring log fire, but also Lottie's beautiful spaniel, Merry.

'I'm so sorry, Sarah. I completely forgot you're allergic,' Asher said, apologising profusely when Terry reminded him that Sarah had a bit of a problem with dogs.

'It seems I'm not the only one.' Molly gave Terry a sardonic smile.

'Don't worry about me.' Sarah was already sniffing but she held up a hand and waved at Asher and Lottie from a distance of a few feet.

'It's lovely to meet you, Lottie,' Terry said, 'and we really don't want to be rude, but I think we'd better go home.' He shook his head, smiled wanly at Asher and Lottie and turned as if to leave, without even sitting down.

'That's the best thing you've said all day.' Molly didn't hide her sarcasm. 'It's lovely to see you again, Asher, and it's great to meet you, Lottie. We must do this again soon. Only possibly, without beautiful Merry in tow.'

'We could ... achoo! ... stay for one ... a-ch-oo! ... drink.' Sarah croaked out the words between sneezes.

Molly snorted in derision. 'You have got to be kidding me. Even if you sat at the other end of the pub, your eyes will be streaming in less than five minutes.'

Lottie leapt to her feet, a contrite expression on her pretty face. 'I'm really sorry about this. I can ask my aunt ... I mean, my mum, if she'll look after Merry, if that helps. I know she won't mind.'

Molly smiled at her. 'That's really kind of you to offer, but I think it's too late. Please don't feel bad about it though. It's not your fault. I also inflicted a dog on Sarah a few days ago. It's just one of those things.'

Sarah sneezed so loudly that everyone in the pub stopped chatting and stared at her. Her eyes were now streaming.

'I'm so ... sorry,' she mumbled. 'Sorry, Lottie. I've ... got to go. I'll be out ... in the fresh ... a-ch-oooo! ... air.' She glanced at Terry and waved goodbye to Asher and Lottie and trudged towards the door, sneezing loudly as she went.

'Sorry mate,' Terry said, his gaze darting to and fro from Sarah to Asher. 'I'll call you later. So sorry about this, Lottie. Hope to see you again soon. Perhaps you can both come round for dinner next week? Only without your dog.'

'That'd be great,' Asher said, giving his girlfriend Lottie a loving and supportive smile.

'But speaking of dogs, Molly, and before you dash off, how's Miracle doing? No one's claimed him yet. And where's he staying if not at Terry and Sarah's?'

Molly opened her mouth to speak, but burst into tears instead, and left Terry to explain the situation as she hurried out after Sarah, into the glaring sunshine.

The rest of the day was a blur, with the assistance of several glasses of wine, a box of chocolates and copious amounts of tears. Molly thought her heart would break when she went in search of more chocolate, and remembered the two bars that Chance had given her.

Finally she'd fallen asleep, but even her dreams were of Chance.

Sunday was no better. Again, the sun burned into her swollen, puffy eyes from first thing in the morning, and she decided the best place to spend the day was tucked up beneath her covers.

Sarah and Terry let her sleep in, but they made her come downstairs for lunch and they even made her change out of her pyjamas.

'I know your heart is breaking,' Sarah said, 'but you still need to get out of bed and go through the motions, however hard that might be.'

'How can this be so painful? That's what I don't understand. I've had a broken heart before, but it's never felt like this. I honestly think I might die.'

Sarah tutted and grabbed her arm. 'That's it. I've heard enough. Get in the shower, get dressed and come downstairs. Molly Ford isn't a quitter. She isn't a loser, either. Yes, this hurts like hell. And it probably will for months to come. The sooner you accept that and deal with it, the better you'll feel in the end.'

Molly wasn't convinced, but she knew Sarah was right. Wallowing wouldn't help. It wouldn't change the situation. And Molly had lived through worse than this. Her beloved dog Belter had died when she was twelve, followed a few months later by her parents. She survived all that. She could survive this.

She didn't really have a choice.

Monday was a little better than Sunday. Today, Molly even appreciated how lovely it was to feel the sunshine on her face as she, Sarah and Terry went out for a short stroll. She had insisted they walked in the opposite direction of both Wishing Well Cottage and Vicky's house, and they hadn't stayed out for long. But at least it was a start.

Tuesday brought news.

Molly wasn't sure at first if it was good or bad, but she was happy to see Vicky standing on Terry's doorstep, although as Vicky had both Beauty and Miracle with her, she couldn't invite Vicky in.

'I know Sarah is allergic,' Vicky said,

smiling brightly. 'But I thought that you should hear this from me. Would you take a walk with us?'

'Us?' Molly's eyes scanned the vicinity in the ridiculous hope that 'us' included Chance. But he was nowhere to be seen.

'I meant me and the dogs,' Vicky said, almost apologising for the fact her son wasn't with her. She clearly knew the way Molly's mind was working.

'Oh. Yes of course. Just give me a minute to get my coat and boots. Hello you two.'

She petted both dogs for a second before hurrying inside and telling Sarah and Terry that she was going out with Vicky and would be back later.

She and Vicky walked in silence for a while.

'How ... How is he?' Molly eventually asked.

Vicky sighed. 'That's what I've come to tell you. He's gone to New York.'

Molly stopped in her tracks, her eyes as wide as Christmas baubles.

'Gone! To New York? When?'

'He left yesterday afternoon. He wouldn't tell me why. All I know is that he was on the phone to Jolene for a long time the night before, and most of yesterday morning. I met a friend for coffee and when I got back, he was already packed and had booked a flight.'

'Is he ... is he coming back?'

Vicky shrugged. 'Search me. He said he will be, but he didn't say when. He told me not to worry and that he didn't want to discuss it yet. He said he'd be in touch but to call if I needed anything. He also apologised for leaving me in the lurch with two dogs, but I told him that wasn't a problem. Nevertheless, he informed me he'd already asked our neighbour's son if he would help out walking the dogs. He even insisted on paying him to do it. He also made me call my friends so that he was sure I'd have company while he was away. And that was it. He made sure I had everything I needed, waited for one of my friends to arrive, then he called a cab, kissed the dogs and me goodbye, and was gone.'

'I ... I can't believe he's left you.'

'To be honest, nor can I. I don't mind, of course. I'm fine on my own and I have my friends, but it's so unlike him. It's as if he's become a different person overnight. My son would never behave like that. I'm not sure what to think. Has something happened? Is Jolene having second thoughts? Is something wrong with the baby? Or with his own father? My ex-husband and I are on speaking terms now, but if something happened to him, Chance would never tell me until he absolutely had to. I don't want to burden you with this, and I certainly don't want you to worry, but I did want you to know he'd left. Just in case you heard about it from someone else. Or came round and found he wasn't there. I was going to call and tell you, but I thought it would be better to break the news face-to-face.'

'Thank you. I appreciate that. I will worry though. But I'm glad I know.'

They resumed their walk in silence, and Vicky linked her arm with Molly's.

'I don't think Miracle swallowing the engagement ring helped.'

'What!'

Molly stopped again and stared at Miracle who was busy smelling a patch of grass.

'Oh. Didn't I say? Sorry, sweetheart. My head is all over the place at the moment. It happened on Sunday morning. Jolene had called. Again. And afterwards, Chance was sitting on the sofa, staring at the ring as it sat in its velvet box. He took it out and twisted it around in his hands, almost as though he wasn't sure what it was. It was all very strange. Although it was a beautiful ring. The next thing I know, he's dropped it. It just seemed to slip through his fingers. Unfortunately, Miracle saw it too. Before Chance could get to it, Miracle had wolfed it down in one loud swallow and smacked his jaws together as if he'd just eaten a piece of prime steak and had really enjoyed it. I laughed of course. Well, in normal circumstances, it would have been funny. Awful too, obviously, but nevertheless quite amusing. Until Chance said the ring might cause an injury to Miracle.'

'Oh my God! Is he okay?'

Molly bent down and took Miracle's head in her hands, staring into his eyes as if hoping he would answer. He promptly licked her face and nuzzled closer.

Vicky laughed. 'He's fine. Look at him. Chance was on the phone to Asher immediately and rushed him over to the surgery. Asher said it would probably work its way through between ten to twenty-four hours, but as it had only just been swallowed, he gave Miracle something to induce vomiting and shortly after, Miracle threw it up. Asher checked him over and pronounced no harm was done and no sooner had Chance brought the poor baby home than Miracle was munching down his lunch as if nothing had happened.'

Molly couldn't help but smile as she stroked and kissed his head.

'And the ring?'

'Asher washed it under the tap, and Chance brought it home.'

'Eew. I hope he doesn't tell ... Jolene what happened to it.' Molly struggled to say her name.

'I told him not to and that what she doesn't know won't hurt her. He just gave me a very odd look and, after washing it again, put it back in its box and changed the subject.'

'And Miracle's definitely okay?'

She tickled him under his chin and rubbed his tummy as he rolled onto his back.

'He's absolutely fine. You can see he is. Asher said it hadn't gone down far and I believe he took an X-Ray. I know that Chance – and Asher, would've done what was best for Miracle. And as I said, he wolfed down his lunch with no problem and he's eaten a lot more since then.'

Molly stood upright and sighed. 'I wish I'd known.'

Vicky shook her head. 'I don't think Chance wanted to worry you. But if he'd thought there was any real danger, I know he would've called you. Or asked Asher to do so. Honestly, sweetheart, there's nothing to worry about. At least not as far as Miracle is concerned. As for Chance. Well. I'll let you know the moment I hear anything. Now I've got to go to the cottage and wait for the rest of his furniture to be delivered. Well, most of it. The bed's not arriving until New Year's Eve. Not that it matters now. He won't be here to use it.'

Molly managed to hold back the tears until Vicky had waved goodbye, but as soon as Vicky and the dogs were out of sight, she ran back to her brother's, raced upstairs, fell on the bed and wept.

Chance had gone back to New York and

she would probably never see him again.

But how could he have left his mum like that?

And Miracle.

And her.

Twenty-Nine

'Have you heard from Vicky?' Sarah asked, the following day, after coming back from a trip to the shops. Although invited, Molly had decided not to join her.

Molly felt herself tense.

'Not since yesterday. No. Why?' She sat upright on the sofa. 'Has he come back? Has he brought her? Has something happened?'

'Not to Chance. No. But I've just seen Vicky and I can't quite believe it. Actually, she did ask me to mention to you that she would give you a call and tell you all about it, so I don't know why I asked if you'd heard from her. It must be because I'm in shock.'

'Why? What is it? For God's sake Sarah, tell me!'

'Vicky's got a boyfriend.'

Molly's mouth fell open but no words came out.

'I know!' Sarah continued: 'I think I did the same. I was gobsmacked. The pair of them were having coffee in The Cherry Topped Café. Apparently, he's been delivering parcels to the cottage since Chance bought the place. Vicky's been there a few times when he's done a delivery, and they struck up a conversation. They talked for longer each time. Yesterday – no doubt after she'd seen you – he turned up with another delivery and she asked him if he had time for a cup of coffee. Apparently, he did. One thing led to another and he texted her this morning and asked her if she'd like to meet for coffee at the café.'

'Really? Are you sure?'

'Yep. Vicky told me herself. And they looked very cosy together, believe me. They were holding hands across the table. I wasn't sure whether to let her know I'd seen them, but she spotted me and beckoned me inside. We chatted for a while and she introduced me to him. His name is Bruce. He's five years older than Vicky, and a widower. He delivers parcels to keep himself occupied. And to keep himself fit. And I have to say, he was rather fit for a man in his late sixties. Quite good looking, too.'

'That's wonderful,' Molly said. Although she couldn't summon up as much enthusiasm as she would have liked. 'At least Chance won't have to worry about her being alone in the coming months. Assuming this leads to more than just a couple of cups of coffee.'

'It already has. She's invited him to her

place for lunch. And this evening, they're taking the dogs for a long walk. He loves dogs, so that helps.'

'Wow. I'm really happy for her.'

'Yes. You sound it. Try to be a little more pleased when she does call you to tell you.'

'I will. I'm sorry. Just one of those days, I'm afraid.'

This was just fabulous news.

Sarah and Terry were engaged. Chance and ... Jolene were about to be, with or without a ring. Now even Vicky had a boyfriend.

Molly was happy for them all. Although maybe not for Jolene. But she couldn't help feeling a little like a loser, without a boyfriend of her own. Perhaps she should phone Mikkel Meloy at The Seahorse Inn and ask if they could drown their sorrows together, after all.

The sad part was, she didn't even fancy alcohol at the moment. And even the thought of chocolate made her feel nauseous. Clearly, you *can* have too much of a good thing.

She paced around the kitchen as she helped Sarah unpack the shopping, until Sarah tutted and rolled her eyes.

'You've just put the teabags in the fridge, Molly.'

'Oh. Have I? Sorry.'

She opened the door and took them back out, this time putting them in the right cupboard. Which is where she found the butter.

And the frozen peas. She glanced at Sarah and smiled sheepishly.

'Why don't you make us both a cup of coffee?' Sarah suggested.

'Are you sure you trust me to do that? You could end up with a mug of watery baked beans the way things are going.'

Sarah gave her a great big hug and led her to one of the kitchen chairs.

'Sit down. I'll make the coffee. I made some cakes earlier. Would you like one?'

'As long as it's not chocolate. And hasn't got chocolate on it, or in it, or anywhere in sight.'

'There's a lemon drizzle cake, four giant coffee eclairs and some more mince pies.'

'Perfect. And what are you having?'

'Yay! You've got your sense of humour back.'

Molly raised her brows. 'No I haven't. I wasn't joking. I could eat them all right now.' But she smiled and winked at Sarah.

Vicky phoned her just before lunch and gave her the lowdown on Bruce.

'He works for one of the big parcel delivery companies. I can't remember which one. I'll ask him later. He's been making a lot of the deliveries to the cottage and we exchanged a few words each time. Then the other day, we got chatting, and he said he used to know someone who had once lived there. I wondered if it was the same people I had known, but it wasn't. But we got into a conversation about the cottage, about Chance, and about lots of other things. Before we knew it, half an hour had flown by. Yesterday, as I was there on my own, I asked if he fancied a coffee. He said he could take a short break and we had lovely chat about the dogs. He had my mobile number because, now that I'm taking the deliveries on behalf of Chance, I get the delivery alerts, so he sent me what he said was a somewhat cheeky text, bearing in mind he was working, and asked if I'd meet him for coffee this morning. As a date. I know this sounds ridiculous, sweetheart, but I really like him already. And the best part is, he is teetotal. I told him about my previous problem and he wasn't in the least bit worried.'

'Does...?'

'Chance know?' Vicky finished the sentence Molly couldn't manage. 'No.' She laughed down the phone. 'I haven't told him yet.'

'Have you heard from him?'

'Yes. Actually I have. Last night. But I'll tell you all about that another time. I've got to run. Bruce will be here soon and he's only got an hour for lunch.'

'Vicky!'

'Yes, sweetheart?'

'I'm really pleased for you. Truly I am. I ...

I hope I get to meet him. Bruce I mean.'

'Thank you, Molly. That means a lot to me. And you'll definitely meet him soon. I know it may not feel like it right now, but I'm pretty certain things will start looking up for you too. Possibly sooner than you think. But I have to go. Lots of love, sweetheart.'

'And to you. Have fun.'

Molly rang off and stared into the mirror in the sitting room.

'Things will start looking up for me. Really? Yeah. And we'll have snow again on New Year's Eve.'

As all the forecasts predicted unusually high temperatures and bright sunny days for today, New Year's Eve, and New Year's Day, snow was extremely unlikely.

Thirty

Today was New Year's Eve and Molly had made a decision. Tomorrow she would be returning home to Bristol. Christmas, and Easterhill, would be miles behind her, both figuratively and factually.

She would allow herself to think about Chance, and what might have been, for today, but that was going to be it. No matter how much her heart was breaking, no matter how much she longed to hear his name, she intended to tell Sarah and Terry that she didn't want to hear about him for at least the next few months. She would also ask Vicky not to mention him to her, if at all possible, for the same amount of time.

Not that Vicky would have any reason to contact her and tell her what he was doing. Prior to this Christmas, the only time Vicky had mentioned him was if she bumped into Molly in the street in Easterhill. As Molly had no intention of returning to Easterhill for at least a couple of months, she wouldn't be bumping into Vicky. They had never texted or called one another before, so why should now be any different?

Except it was. They had grown close this Christmas. Vicky had made her feel as if she were a part of the family. And Vicky would be looking after Miracle. Molly wanted to know how he was doing. But Vicky could tell Sarah that, and Sarah could tell Molly.

It would just make it easier if she didn't have to hear Vicky's voice. It reminded her far too much of Chance. Not that he sounded like his mum. He didn't. But it was just some of the things she said, and the way she said them, that brought back memories Molly would rather not have to deal with.

Molly got out of bed and drew back the curtains. She couldn't believe her eyes. Instead of the sunshine the forecasters had predicted, the sky was a mass of clouds. Banks of clouds. And not just any clouds. These clouds looked remarkably like the ones that had brought blizzards of snow for days on end over Christmas.

How could the forecasts have been so wrong? But it wasn't the first time and it probably wouldn't be the last.

Even as she watched the clouds tumble across the sky, banging into one another like fluffy dodgem cars, the first heavy snowflakes began to fall.

By the time she had showered, dressed and gone downstairs, a layer of snow already covered the pavement, the garden, the houses and the trees.

'It's snowing!'

'Now who's the ace detective?' Terry asked, drolly.

Molly pulled a face.

'Very funny. The forecast was for sunshine. Lots and lots of sunshine. And unseasonably high temperatures.'

'It appears it was wrong.'

'Yes but ... I'm leaving tomorrow.'

'And?'

Molly sighed. 'And, brother dear, if this snow is as bad as last time, I might get stuck here. Perhaps I should go right now? Just in case.'

'You can't do that.' Sarah seemed genuinely upset.

'Why not?'

Terry tutted. 'Because it's New Year's Eve.'

'And?' She glanced at Terry and grinned.

'And we have plans. We're going to The Piemaker's Rest.'

'Yes,' Sarah said. 'We always go there on New Year's Eve.'

'I think this year you may have to go without me. I'm sorry, Sarah. I can't risk being stuck here for days on end. I've got a business to run.'

'You can run that from anywhere. You already do a lot of it online. Okay, I accept a number of your clients and suppliers are based in and around Bristol, but it's a big wide world, Molly and people in Easterhill and all the surrounding towns and villages need interior designers just as much as the people in Bristol do. Chance proved that.'

'Can we please not mention his name? I was going to ask you a big favour. I know it may seem silly, but can we please not speak of him again for the foreseeable future?'

Sarah and Terry stared at one another before looking back at her.

'Are you serious?' Terry asked.

'Deadly.'

'But he's my friend.'

'And he can remain your friend. I'm not asking you not to see him, or talk to him. I'm asking you not to tell me about it. That's all. Or to mention what he's up to. I need to get over him. I need to move on. And I can't do that if I keep hearing his name every five seconds.'

'Okay,' Sarah said, nodding. 'We can do that. We can, can't we darling?'

'I suppose so. If it helps.' Terry nodded. 'Okay, Molly. We'll never mention him again from this moment on. Until you tell us we can.'

'Thank you so much. You two are the best.'

'So are you staying?' Sarah queried.

Molly looked out of the window as the snow fell thick and fast.

She shook her head. 'I think I need to leave. Look at it.'

'Stay,' Sarah pleaded. 'Please stay. Tomorrow's a bank holiday and then it's the weekend. You can leave on Sunday. The snow might have gone by then.'

That was true. And no one was going to be working over this holiday. She could return to Bristol in January. No harm would be done.

'Okay. I'll stay. But I'm not sure I'm up to going to the pub tonight.'

'So you won't make an effort, even for us?' Terry asked.

Molly felt guilty and sighed.

'I'll try. But I may not be very good company tonight.'

'Who told you you ever are?' Terry said, laughing.

'Do you want to live to see the New Year in?' Molly asked. But she laughed too.

'I think we should go shopping,' Sarah said.

'You went shopping yesterday.' Terry rolled his eyes.

'Not that sort of shopping, darling. Fun shopping. Just Molly and me.'

'I'm not sure I'm in the mood to go shopping, Sarah. And it's snowing, remember?'

'I know. So let's go now, before it gets too

bad.'

'I don't want to.'

'Molly Ford. Stop being such a bloody misery. It's New Year's Eve. Tomorrow is a whole new start. Let's go and buy something fabulous to wear tonight to show next year that we mean business.'

Molly liked the sound of that. It was a positive step. A powerful step. The sort of thing all those self-help books tell you you should do.

'Okay. Fine. I'll get my coat.'

Thirty-One

Molly's heart hadn't really been in the whole shopping experience, especially as it seemed everyone in Easterhill had had the same idea. The shopping centre was packed and it had taken half an hour to get out of the car park, partly due to the crowds but also because of the weather.

But she had bought another rather stunning dress. From the same shop as the last one, as it happened. Which brought back all sorts of memories and took her to places she really didn't want to go right now. Like memories of the way Chance had looked at her on Christmas Eve. And the way he had kissed her later that night.

Now, as she studied her reflection in her bedroom mirror, all those same memories came flooding back once more. She shook her head in the hope of sending them away, but it didn't work completely. All it did was make her updo looser and set free several strands of her wavy, golden apricot hair. Not that she cared. All she could think about now was Chance. She could picture his handsome face so clearly, and she thought her heart would break all over again.

This wasn't the way to start her New Year's Eve.

She ran her hands over the tight-fitting, electric-blue dress and turned from side to side. Apart from her face looking paler than usual and her eyes not quite as bright, she didn't look bad for someone with a broken heart.

Her phone pinged and she read the text. She was surprised to see it was from Vicky.

'So sorry. Emergency at the cottage. Can you come right away? Xx'

Molly stared at it as if the text contained some sort of dreadful, contagious virus.

Why on earth would Vicky ask her to go to the cottage? Especially on New Year's Eve. What sort of emergency could there be? And if it was a real emergency, would she really have added two kisses?

Molly ran downstairs and showed the text to Sarah and Terry.

'What do you think it means?'

'I think it means Vicky wants you to go to the cottage pretty damn quick,' Terry said, somewhat unhelpfully.

'No kidding, Sherlock. What I mean is, why

would she ask me to go?'

'Have you texted her back and asked her?' Sarah suggested.

'Er. No. That didn't actually occur to me.'

'I always said my sister was a genius.'

'Oh shut up, you. I'll text her now.'

Molly sent her a text saying, 'Hi Vicky. Was that text meant for me? I'm sure you know that the cottage is the last place I want to be. Is everything okay? Xx'

A text pinged back almost immediately.

'Sorry. I wouldn't ask unless I had to. Please come, Molly. ASAP. Really urgent. I need you here.'

'Okay. That's weird,' Sarah said. 'Oh my God! You don't think Bruce is some sort of maniac and that he's kidnapped her and is holding her to ransom or something, do you?'

Molly raised her eyebrows, stared at her friend, and laughed.

'No, Sarah. I don't. And if he was, she would text her son, not us.'

'Good point.'

'It is a bit odd though,' Terry added. 'Why doesn't she just tell you what's wrong?'

'I'll ask her.'

Molly sent another text simply saying, 'What's wrong?'

A second later her phone rang and she saw it was Vicky calling.

'For God's sake, Molly! What do I have to

do to get you here? I could be dying, sweetheart. If you care about me at all, come right now. I really, really need you here.' And then she rang off.

Molly stared at Sarah and Terry in disbelief.

'Well, that was really strange. Bloody hell. You don't think Bruce has dumped her and she's gone back to the bottle?'

Terry sighed. 'That's about as daft as Sarah's suggestion. I've got an idea. Why don't you go to the cottage and find out what she wants?' His voice dripped sarcasm.

'Because, brother dear, that bloody cottage is not somewhere I want to be on New Year's Eve.'

'Five minutes wouldn't hurt you, surely?'

'Terry does have a point.' Sarah looked thoughtful. 'The sooner you go, the sooner you'll be back and we can go to the pub.'

'Or you could come with me.'

Sarah and Terry exchanged glances again.

'We could do that,' Terry said. 'And I'm happy to, if it'll put an end to this stupid conversation.' He got up from his chair and walked towards the door. 'Come on then.'

'Right now?' Sarah asked.

'Isn't it supposed to be an emergency?' Terry rolled his eyes.

'I wish you'd stop doing that,' Molly said, grabbing her coat and bag and slipping her phone inside the front pocket. 'Oh no. I've just thought of something. You don't think something's happened to Miracle, do you? And that's why she wouldn't tell me? Because that's not the sort of news you break over the phone, and certainly not via text.'

'Oh hell.' Terry looked worried.

So did Sarah. 'I truly hope not. Let's go.'

Sarah grabbed her coat and all three of them rushed out into the snow.

'I'll drive,' Terry said, getting in the driver's seat.

A second later, they sped off towards Wishing Well Cottage.

Thirty-Two

'At least we know the place hasn't burnt down,' Terry said, as they pulled up outside just a couple of minutes later.

The curtains were drawn tight, but a warm glow seeped through a few chinks in the material and a rainbow of colour reflected on the snow-covered front garden from the myriad fairy lights around the doors and windows.

'That's not very funny.'

Molly got out of the car, took a deep breath, and made her way gingerly across the snowy path, to the front door. Her thigh-high leather boots kept her warm in this weather, but the soles weren't great for snowy conditions.

As she neared the door, she couldn't help but smile at the beautiful wreath she and Chance had made. It was full of white-painted pine cones, white winter roses, silver glittery sprayed leaves and twigs, and tied in a soft-grey, sparkly ribbon to match the warm-grey paintwork.

She knocked on the door and rang the bell, just for good measure.

The door burst open and Vicky stood inside, arm in arm with a handsome, grey-haired man, who looked to be in his late sixties.

'Hello, sweetheart. This is Bruce. Happy New Year's Eve.'

What the hell was going on?

'Hello, Molly,' Bruce said. 'I've heard a lot about you. It's lovely to meet you.'

'Er. Hi Bruce.' Molly smiled at him and glanced around at Sarah and Terry who were walking up the path, and just a little way behind her. 'It's lovely to meet you too.'

Sarah and Terry looked as confused as she was.

'Don't stand out there in the cold,' Vicky said. 'Come inside and get warm.'

'Er. Sorry Vicky. But what on earth is going on? I may be wrong, but I get the feeling there isn't an emergency.'

'Actually, there is.'

Molly recognised the voice immediately. It was Chance. He was here. He was in this cottage. Right now. And it was New Year's Eve.

Holy crap!

Molly screwed up her eyes. Please, please don't let this be happening.

Had Vicky arranged some sort of New Year's Eve party-cum-engagement celebration for Chance and Jolene, and actually invited Molly to it? Surely no one was that insane?

Vicky and Bruce stepped aside as Sarah and Terry reached Molly's side.

'Is that Chance?'

Sarah pointed towards the figure in the hall. He was standing in shadow but it was obvious to all that it was him.

'What's he doing here?' Terry said. 'I thought he was in New York.'

'So did I,' Molly said, turning away from the door.

'Molly! Don't go.' It was Vicky who said that.

'Please don't,' Chance added. 'There's something I need to say to you.'

She turned to face him and scowled at Vicky, Bruce, and him.

'What could you possibly have to say to me that I want to hear?'

'I don't know if you do want to hear it. But I really hope you do. How about if I start with, I'm sorry?'

'Not as sorry as I am.'

She turned away again.

'What if I said I never meant to hurt you?'

She spun on her heel and glared at him.

'And that makes everything okay?'

'No.' He stepped forward into the light and smiled. 'It doesn't. But I'm hoping that this might.'

He took a small, velvet covered box from his pocket and she gasped and took a step back.

'You're going to show me your engagement ring? The ring you're about to give to your girlfriend. Your pregnant girlfriend, I might add. Thanks. But I really don't want to see it. Especially as it's been in Miracle's throat and covered in his vomit. Oh God. I don't suppose she knows that, does she? I honestly didn't mean to blurt that out. I can't be here. I need to leave. Goodbye. Good luck. Happy bloody New Year to one and all.'

'Molly!' Chance sounded a little cross. 'Okay. Maybe this wasn't such a good idea. It seemed so much better in my head. But for your information, this isn't the ring that Miracle swallowed. I took that back to the jewellers and told them what had happened. They're having it professionally cleaned and they gave me a really good price, all things considered. And Jolene isn't here. I'm not planning to propose to her tonight. Or ever. Thankfully, she discovered the other day that she isn't, in fact, pregnant. It was a false alarm. If she'd waited a couple of days, none of this would've happened. But she genuinely thought she was and she wanted to tell me on Christmas Day. She was under the impression I'd be thrilled.'

'And weren't you?'

He shook his head. 'Surely you know the

answer to that? As soon as I knew I wasn't going to be a dad, and that I didn't have to stay with her, I went to New York to tell her face to face that it was over between us. Because that's just not the sort of thing you should do by text, or phone, or video call. And if you would stop scowling at me for a second and really look at me, you might realise that I'm standing here and offering you my love, my heart, my home, and everything else I have to give you. Including a new ring that I bought in New York before I left today, just for you. Because I love you and I want you to be my wife more than I've ever wanted anything.'

'Bloody hell,' Sarah said. 'That was almost as good as your proposal, darling.' She smiled lovingly at Terry.

Molly turned to Sarah and Terry and mouthed the words, 'Did he just say he wants to marry me?' Only she said them out loud as well.

'He did.' Sarah nodded and beamed at her.

'Yep,' Terry said, a huge grin spreading across his face.

'I did,' Chance said, his voice cracking with emotion. 'I do. I love you with all my heart. I think I've always loved you. I just didn't realise that until this Christmas.'

Molly turned to face him and saw the smile and the tears of joy on Vicky's face. Even Bruce looked emotional. In a good way. They both stepped aside.

'We'll leave you two to it,' Vicky said, kissing Chance on the cheek. 'Happy New Year's Eve, darling. Good luck. Not that I think you'll need it. Bruce and I are going back to mine. The dogs are waiting.'

'Happy New Year's Eve, Mum. And thanks for everything.'

Vicky and Bruce walked towards Molly, hand in hand and beamed at her as they did so.

'Happy New Year's Eve, sweetheart.' Vicky kissed her on the cheek just as she had done to Chance. But she also winked at Molly. 'Please say yes. I feel you are already family, but I'd quite like to make it official.'

'We'll go too,' Sarah said. 'You know where we'll be if you need us. Not that I think you will. Have fun. We love you.' She turned to look at Chance. 'Don't you dare mess this up, or you'll have us to answer to.'

'I promise you, the last thing I want to do is mess this up.' He smiled at them before turning his attention back to Molly.

'You had better be serious about this, mate,' Terry said.

Chance held Molly's gaze as he answered his friend. 'I am. I'm deadly serious.'

'Okay. See you later then. Happy New Year's Eve.'

Sarah and Terry kissed Molly on the cheek and waved at Chance but neither Molly nor

Chance paid any attention. They were too busy gazing at one another.

'Are you coming in?' Chance asked. 'Or do I have to go down on one knee on the doorstep?'

'Are you ... are you seriously proposing to me?'

'Er. That was the plan. I thought I was. Don't you want me to?'

'The plan was to propose to Jolene tonight, not me.'

'Ah. I see your point. I should've chosen another venue, shouldn't I? Or another night? The thing is, Molly. I've just flown back from New York. I only arrived about an hour ago. To be honest, I'm not quite sure what's going on in my head. But I am sure of one thing. And that is, that I love you with all of my heart. And that I want to marry you, and spend my life with you. And I want that to start as soon as possible. Okay, that's possibly three things. Maybe four. But there're all rolled into one in my head and my heart.'

Molly tried to contain her excitement.

'Oh really? And do I have any say in this matter?'

'Er. Yes. Of course. Are you ... are you saying you don't feel the same way about me? Because I was pretty sure you did. And Mum is certain of it. But if I've misjudged the situation, please tell me now. It won't change the way I feel. And I'll still propose. I'll do everything I can to make you fall in love with me, if you haven't done so. I'm quite a good guy. I know you might not believe that, bearing in mind I kissed you when I had another girlfriend. Twice. But I swear to you, that's not something I've ever done before, or ever will again. I only did that because it was you, Molly. That sounds lame, doesn't it? But it's the truth. And the thing is, I really can't imagine my life without you. I honestly can't.'

She couldn't do it to him. She couldn't make him worry that she might not feel for him what he obviously felt for her.

'It's a good thing that I love you too then, isn't it? That I want to spend my life with you. And I can't wait for that to start.'

'So ... you do love me? Really love me?'

'I do really love you. Really. Really. Really love you. But I want a proper proposal. And not outside, here in the snow. I'm freezing!'

He beamed at her, slipped the ring and the box back into his trouser pocket, dashed to her and swept her into his arms, carrying her into the hall where he stood her on her feet and kissed her.

His kiss was better than both his previous kisses had been. It was deeper. It was more passionate. It made her feel as if she were floating on air, or dancing in moonlight. It made her feel as if she were the most beautiful woman on this earth. It sent all sorts of sensations rushing through her. And when he eventually released her, took her hand and led her along the hall, she knew that all her hopes and wishes and dreams were about to become reality.

'Chance?'

'Yes, Molly.'

'Before you propose properly, there's just one little thing I need to know.'

He tipped his head to one side and looked her directly in the eye.

'What's that? I'll tell you anything you want and I'll be completely honest.'

'Do you have a bed? Because if you think I'm sleeping on the floor, I'm not. Not even with the man I adore.'

His face was a picture as he roared with laughter and happiness.

'It just so happens, the bed was delivered today. Mum and Bruce were here and took delivery. I believe Mum has even washed the brand new sheets you chose, and made the bed up with them. But – and forgive me if I'm wrong here, I was rather hoping that sleeping wasn't something we'd be doing a lot of tonight, new bed or not.'

'You're not wrong, Chance. You're absolutely right. And if I might make a suggestion, could we possibly save the proposal until midnight? That way you'll have proposed to me this year and also next year too.'

'I think that's a brilliant suggestion.'

'And in the meantime, why don't we go and try out your new bed? We may not be able to see the stars but we can watch the falling snow instead.'

He grinned at her. 'That's also a brilliant suggestion.'

'And when I say, watch the falling snow, you do realise I mean after we've got naked and had at least three hours of passionate sex, don't you?'

'That's exactly what I was hoping, Molly. But why stop at three hours? After all, we've got all night. And once you've said, yes, we'll have the rest of our lives.'

'I definitely love the sound of that. Just one more thing.'

'Yes?'

'May I see the ring again, please?'

'Nope. Not until I propose properly. You said that was what you wanted. Which reminds me. I left the champagne in an ice bucket on the kitchen island. I'll just go and grab it.'

'You can grab it later, Chance. Right now, I really need you to grab me. And when I say grab, what I mean is—'

'I think I know exactly what you mean, Molly. I may not be much good at interior design but there are a few things I do know how to do, especially on a brand new bed.'

'Excellent. Oh wait! I've thought of something else I need to ask.'

He laughed and shook his head. 'What's that?'

'Does this mean that we'll be living here? Because I really want to live here. I adore this cottage almost as much as I adore you.'

'I was really hoping you'd say that. But what about your business? Can you run that from here?'

'I can run it from anywhere. And as Sarah told me, people in Easterhill need interior designers just as much as people in Bristol.'

'I totally agree with that.'

'Oh. Just one final thing.'

He pulled her into his arms and his blue eyes sparkled with love and laughter and happiness.

'Yes, my darling Molly. What is it?'

'Does this mean we can adopt Miracle?'

He laughed even more. 'Absolutely. Although I think we may have to share him with Mum and Beauty.'

'I'm okay with that. Happy New Year's Eve, Chance.'

'Happy New Year's Eve, Molly. I'm looking forward to a lifetime of New Year's Eves with you. Anything else you want to ask?'

She shook her head and beamed at him. 'Nope. Other than, when am I going to see your new bed?'

'Right now.'

He swept her into his arms once more and carried her upstairs to the master bedroom. The bedroom Molly had designed in both of their favourite colours: pink and blue. Almost as if she knew that she would be sleeping in it with Chance.

But then, she did always pride herself on the fact that, deep down, she always knew exactly what her clients wanted. It just so happened that this time, it was what she wanted too.

Coming soon

My next book is book 3 in my standalone, Seahorse Harbour novels. We're currently deciding on the title and I'll have exciting news about that very soon.

Check out my website for details or follow me on social media.

If you love my books, sign up for my newsletter, or join my exclusive, Facebook group. Details are on the next page. You'll be the first to hear all my news and you might even win a free gift in one of my regular giveaways.

A Note from Emily

Thank you for reading this book. If you loved it and want to be the first to find out about my new books, and also, chat with me and other fans, ask to join the exclusive Emily Harvale's Readers' Club Facebook group. Or go to: www.emilyharvale.com and subscribe to my newsletter via the 'Sign me up' box.

A little piece of my heart goes into all my books and when I send them on their way, I really hope they bring a smile to someone's face. If this book made you smile, or gave you a few pleasant hours of relaxation, I'd be delighted if you'd tell your friends.
I'd also love it if you have a minute or two to post a review. Just a few words will do, and a kind review makes such a difference to my day – to any author's day. Huge thanks to those of you who do so, and for your lovely comments and support on social media. Thank you.
A writer's life can be lonely at times. Sharing a virtual cup of coffee or a glass of wine, or exchanging a few friendly words on Facebook, Twitter or Instagram is so much fun.

I mentioned my newsletter just now. It's absolutely free, your email address is safe and won't be shared and I won't bombard you, I promise. You can enter competitions and enjoy some giveaways. In addition to that, there's my author page on Facebook and there's also my lovely, Facebook group. You can chat with me and with other fans and get access to my book news, snippets from my daily life, early extracts from my books and lots more besides. Details are on my website but you'll find all my contact links in the Contact section following this.

I'm working on my next book right now. Let's see where my characters take us this time. Hope to chat with you soon. In the meantime, I'm sending you love and virtual hugs. I can't wait to bring you more stories that I hope will capture your heart, mind and imagination, allowing you to escape into a world of romance in some enticingly beautiful settings.

To see details of my other books, please go to the books page on my website, or scan the QR code below to see all my books on Amazon.

Stay in touch with

Emily Harvale

If you want to be one of the first to hear Emily's news, find out about book releases, see covers, and enter free competitions, then sign up to her Readers' Club by visiting:

www.emilyharvale.com

and subscribing to her newsletter via the 'Sign me up' box. If you love Emily's books and want to chat with her and other fans, ask to join the exclusive

Emily Harvale's Readers' Club Facebook group

Or come and say 'Hello' on social media:

 @EmilyHarvaleWriter

 @EmilyHarvale

 @EmilyHarvale

Acknowledgements

My grateful thanks go to the following:

Christina Harkness for her patience and care in editing this book.
My webmaster, David Cleworth who does so much more than website stuff.
My cover design team, JR.
Luke Brabants. Luke is a talented artist and can be found at: www.lukebrabants.com
My wonderful friends for their friendship and love. You know I love you all.
All the fabulous members of my Readers' Club. You help and support me in so many ways and I am truly grateful for your ongoing friendship. I wouldn't be where I am today without you.
My Twitter and Facebook friends, and fans of my Facebook author page. It's great to chat with you. You help to keep me (relatively) sane!

Printed in Great Britain
by Amazon

50835131R00163